THE GUIDE FOR A SINGLE WOMAN

THE GUIDE FOR A SINGLE WOMAN

AARON GOLDFARB

FG PRESS | BOULDER, COLORADO

The Guide for a Single Woman
©2014 Aaron Goldfarb

All rights reserved. No part of this publication may be reproduced, stored, or transmitted in any form or by any means, electronic, mechanical, photocopying, recording, scanning, or otherwise, without written permission from the publisher. It is illegal to copy this book, post it to a website, or distribute it by any other means without permission.

ART DIRECTOR | Kevin Barrett Kane

EDITOR | Dave Heal

COVER PHOTOGRAPHER | Dane McDonald

COVER PHOTOGRAPH LOCATION
License No. 1, Liquor Bar
in the HOTEL BOULDERADO
2115 13th St.
Boulder, CO
WWW.LICENSE1BOULDERADO.COM

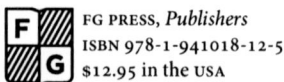

FG PRESS, *Publishers*
ISBN 978-1-941018-12-5
$12.95 in the USA

OTHER TITLES BY AARON GOLDFARB

The Guide for a Single Man

How to Fail: The Self-Hurt Guide

The Cheat Sheet

Drunk Drinking

Inspired by Craig.

Facilitated by Phil.

Dedicated to Betsy.

TABLE OF CONTENTS

1   CHAPTER ONE
Everything Happens for a Reason

6   CHAPTER TWO
It's Not Me It's Me

11   CHAPTER THREE
Single at the Same Time

18   CHAPTER FOUR
Last Date

24   CHAPTER FIVE
Comment Sense

31   CHAPTER SIX
Together Alone

39   CHAPTER SEVEN
Restaurant Weak

45   CHAPTER EIGHT
Searching for the Cliché

54   CHAPTER NINE
The Hierarchy of The One

58   CHAPTER TEN
2014 BC

64   CHAPTER ELEVEN
Only the Bride Cares About Her Wedding

68   CHAPTER TWELVE
Gross Chicks

75   CHAPTER THIRTEEN
Book Clubbed

80   CHAPTER FOURTEEN
Sitcom Situations

87   CHAPTER FIFTEEN
How to Know When a Woman is About to Dump You

90   CHAPTER SIXTEEN
Social Queues

TABLE OF CONTENTS

CHAPTER SEVENTEEN 94
The Only Pick-Up Line That Matters

CHAPTER EIGHTEEN 98
The Night of Many Stands

CHAPTER NINETEEN 102
Hos Before Bros

CHAPTER TWENTY 107
The Year of Being Ridiculous

CHAPTER TWENTY-ONE 113
The Girl With the Dragged-On Taboo

CHAPTER TWENTY-TWO 120
Spec

CHAPTER TWENTY-THREE 126
Contextual

CHAPTER TWENTY-FOUR 133
Sleeping With Him While He's Sleeping

CHAPTER TWENTY-FIVE 140
The Experts

CHAPTER TWENTY-SIX 147
Sex and/or the City

CHAPTER TWENTY-SEVEN 153
The Dangerous Lives of Women

CHAPTER TWENTY-EIGHT 158
What Men Want

CHAPTER TWENTY-NINE 165
Slut Phase

CHAPTER THIRTY 171
The Days of Our LOLives

CHAPTER THIRTY-ONE 177
Describing the Indescribable

ABOUT THE GUIDES

The Guide for a Single Woman is the first of its kind. Not a sequel, not a prequel, but an *equal*. Its counterpart is *The Guide for a Single Man*. Two novels that can be read in either order or completely by themselves in order to learn the full story of two men and two women, and one night in New York.

THE MAP

- **P.J.'s Pub** (w. 58th St. and Broadway)
- **Sven** (Columbus Circle)
- **Belle Époque** (w. 58th St. and Eighth Ave.)
- **Twins** (w. 53rd St. and Broadway)
- **Drunx Pub** (w. 52nd St. & Eleventh Ave.)
- **Duane Reade** (w. 50th St. and Broadway)
- **Patti's** (w. 52nd St. and Broadway)
- **Rudy's** (w. 44th St. and Ninth Ave.)
- **Bloopers** (w. 43rd St. and Eleventh Ave.)
- **Perdition** (w. 49th St. and Tenth Ave.)
- **On the Rocks** (w. 49th St. and Tenth Ave.)
- **J. Mac's** (w. 57th St. and Eleventh Ave.)
- **Flaming Saddles** (w. 53rd St. and Ninth Ave.)

"Loneliness and frustration, we both came down with an acute case…"

-Warren Zevon, "The French Inhaler"

📍 **P.J.'s Pub** (W. 58th St. and Broadway) | 5:12 PM

chapter one
EVERYTHING HAPPENS FOR A REASON

How did we get here?

You and me.

How did we get—

Look, I know you hate these talks. Fine, get your jokes out. We got here…?

"By a smelly cab."

Nice.

"By a smelly cab with a smelly driver who took us to this smelly bar."

Funny. Well your tip also stunk. Yeah, I saw. That was a poor tip even converted to rupees.

But, seriously, how did we get here?

I wish you'd just tell me things, Sweetie. Then, I wouldn't need to piece together your backstory. Either through Google stalking or those rare bits you're actually willing to share. Other bits suppressed either 'cause you're hiding something…or simply 'cause you claim the details are too boring.

They're not boring to me. Nothing about you is boring to me.

Of course I've Googled you!

Let's see…you were born in Kansas City in 1979 and grew up there until you left in 1996. You went to college up here. You were raised by distant parents, but, despite that, you surely had a better childhood than 99% of all people in the world today. Mine was probably better than 99.9%. But you already know my bits and pieces. All of them.

I was born at Mass General and grew up in the Rhode Island suburbs where I went to a small enough school I could be both valedictorian and popular. Invited to cool parties, yet win science fairs. Where I could be All-Conference in basketball and homecoming queen. (You've seen the pictures. I looked ridiculous getting that sash put over my sweaty jersey.) My life as a kid was pretty darn perfect. A prostate cancer scare for Dad, my cat Charcoal accidentally backed over by Mom's station wagon, sure, but those were just bumps in the road of my charmed childhood.

So should we even begin with you and me? Should you ever start with "you and me"?

Instead, let's start with your dad. Scott, right? What if he'd never met your mother? Meryl, correct? Pretty name. I hope to meet them someday.

What if your dad had been infertile? Or your mom barren? What if you'd been given up for adoption? Or…terminated? Your parents were struggling when you were born, right? What if they had gotten divorced before you'd even been conceived… instead of just four years later?

We could go back to your Grandfather Jay. What if he'd died in Korea? Or your great-grandfather, Saul. OK, so I might have played around on Ancestry.com. But, what if Saul had been turned away at Ellis Island, sent back to Poland? What if he'd died of polio? What if Jonas Salk had never been born? Then we might not be here, you and me.

What if you had died in that car accident at nine? Your mom's minivan flips on the highway yet you all just walk away? Nothing more than a few bruises and a sizable settlement from Toyota?

What if your mother had spent that settlement on a Disneyland vacation instead of using it to move you into a nicer school district? (When are you going to take me back to visit?) What if your high school sweetheart hadn't gotten that abortion? You say you weren't "sweethearts," but if you get a high school girl pregnant, she's gonna be your sweetheart for the rest of time. Now you'd be watching your sixteen-year-old son play under Friday night lights instead of drinking some Friday night light beers with me.

Yeah, this beer sucks, we really should have gone some place else.

Luckily for us, I guess, the pregnancy was terminated and your sweetheart became your sweet-not and now you're my Sweetie.

What if NYU had given you a scholarship? You'd have attended.

What if you'd followed your friends to that crappy state school? Four years of partying and now you'd live in St. Louis or Dallas. You'd wear golf shirts and khakis every day of your life.

What if you'd been a frat boy? You might be married to some airhead who still sleeps in shorts with Greek letters on the butt.

What if you'd accepted that entry-level job in Chicago? You'd be dating some girl with a thick accent and thick meat on her bones. You might be a Cubs fan. You might be that Steve Bartman guy. You'd be in hiding and I never would have met you.

What if you'd used Match or eHarmony or even JDate? I know you're not Jewish, but non-Jews still like to use it to find hot little Jews like me. But, what if we both didn't use the dating website we did? What if some surely virginal nerd in his Silicon Valley garage hadn't invented that site? What if a VC hadn't given the surely virginal nerd enough funding and he was forced to fold up shop before we ever had a chance to use it? What if just one of us hadn't had the courage to use online dating? Then there'd never be you and me.

Millions, if not billions of things had to happen for you to find yourself here with me at this smelly little pub on Columbus Circle. Even Columbus had to discover America, or wherever this is, for *this* to happen. Manhattan could still be a forest, still owned by Native Americans and never sold for beads, this place where we currently sit.

Another billion, if not trillions of things had to happen for me to find myself here sitting with you.

Did you know I nearly joined Teach for America out of college? Then what? Get accepted, get sent to North Dakota or Hawaii…*or Peru*, and all of the sudden nothing will ever be the same. I'd be dating some vegan hippie who wears Toms on his feet and Tom's under his armpits and goes to Burning Man every single year.

Did you know I was mugged that summer I lived in Bushwick? What if he had killed me? Or scared me so much I moved back home? I nearly did. My mother begged me to.

Did you know I nearly didn't do online dating because I thought the sites would be full of cheap hipsters with bad beards? And, you know, it *was*. For the first seventeen dates I was batting 0.000. No good first dates, certainly no seconds, no hugs, no kisses, no nothing. A lot of free meals at crappy bars… but that was it.

Then, date eighteen: You.

And I was date one for you.

(So you say.)

That sounds even more amazing, more unlikely.

What if you assumed it would only get better from there and decided to go on more dates? Even just to see if other chicks were as easy as me. Maybe you did. Maybe you still are…?

I know you aren't. Don't worry, Sweetie, I was only kidding. But why haven't you deleted your online profile? You could use that $14.99 a month to buy me a nice cocktail tonight.

Don't worry. I know you have your reasons.

I know you think this is silly.

I know you don't believe everything happens for a reason.

You believe in strategy, not fate.

You believe you seduced me using brilliant strategy. You did this and then that which then caused me to do that and then this.

You think years of "experience," trial and error, and some impeccable strategy brought you to a point where I was just another girl in the layup line of taking New York City girls to bed. If you only knew, Sweetie.

You believe in strategy and sex.

I believe in fate and love.

We were meant to be together.

You didn't need to use strategy.

How could it not be fate when I've just shown you how many thing had to perfectly happen for us to get to this point? I was always meant to meet you and sleep with you and be with you and love you.

Then again, you being a charming and witty guy who uses strategy was meant to be too. The strategy was secondary, though, just a part of our fate.

Me and you. You and me? It was meant to be. It was fate that got us to the point where I will now be the first to say it, six months into our relationship:

"I love you."

That's nice to hear back. I know you love me. You say it whenever you're drunk. But that doesn't count. This does and that just did.

I love you, Sweetie.

Now you're embarrassed. I know you don't like when I get like this.

But I do love you so so much.

Oooh…that's Erin, she's finally out of work.

OK, Sweetie, goodbye. Will I see you later tonight?

Of course I will. I'll see you every tonight for the rest of my nights.

◉ Sven (Columbus Circle) | 5:38 PM

chapter two
IT'S NOT ME IT'S ME

"How are you, hon'?"

We hugged as Erin hopped on the barstool next to mine.

"Not well."

She was a total mess. Sure, she looked cute and put together, but she always did. I knew she was hurting deeply on the inside. She'd just been dumped. By herself.

"What can I do for you?"

"I just need a drink. And to talk."

"Of course."

She swiveled her head back and forth around Sven, a semi-swank pseudo-Nordic cocktail lounge at the top of the Time Warner Center.

"There are some…cute guys here."

I had assumed that, what Erin needed tonight, was to *not* be hit on. But I also realized that, unfortunately, Midtown didn't have many bars two women could meet at for a drink and *not* get hit on. Then again, I suppose no New York City neighborhood—Chelsea included—had the kinds of bars where we would not get hit on.

Men in New York were vultures. Especially on a drunken Friday night. We could have met for a quick glass of Manischewitz at Emanuel Synagogue and next thing you knew, some ancient parishioner named Maury or Mel or Stanley would sidle up to us—as much as a person could sidle up using a walker with tennis balls on the end—and try to turn us into his next trophy wife. Or, at least, next trophy nurse.

That's why I had picked Sven. With it being hard to find, requiring an elevator to reach, having no happy hour specials or TVs (and on the night of a pretty big Knicks game no less), I figured the chances of men being in this bar were slim. I was wrong. There were plenty of men in the bar. Who were all slim.

"Do you want to talk to any of these guys?"

"No. I guess not. I just want…to talk."

A bartender strolled over to us.

"Getcha a drink?"

"Do you know how to make a Moscow Mule?"

"No, but I have an app that does."

At Sven all the bartenders looked like they might also be Sven. Tall, pale, blonde, sinewy. I'm not sure if it was an intentional gimmick or just a coincidence, but you looked behind the bar and saw a lot of young men with great-grandfathers who were probably Vikings.

"Cher', dumping someone is even worse than being dumped."

"Oh? How'd Joe take it?"

"Joe? Who cares about Joe?!"

"You just said—"

"Joe took it…well."

Women always do the dumping in relationships. Even when a man does the dumping, it was almost always orchestrated by the woman. Sometimes the woman didn't even realize this, but, believe me, she had wanted things to end and intentionally torpedoed the relationship.

"He even said I was probably right to dump him. 'Probably right.' He couldn't even say I *was* right. Or that he was sorry. Or that he wished things were different. He just said I was 'probably right.'"

"Any tears?"

Erin exhaled a small laugh, masking a sniffle.

"From Joe or me?!"

I'd seen men *not* cry over the most heart-breaking things (a relative passing, a deprived child, an elderly person struggling with their last breaths), yet bawl over the lame sidenotes of life (sports victories, old timey war documentaries, any movie about a fictional dog croaking).

"No, Joe didn't cry. He smirked though." She thought about it. "That kind of irked me."

"The smirk irked?"

"Him not crying and saying I was 'probably right' actually made me wonder if I'd just made a mistake."

"You *didn't*. You know men and their stupid strategies. He probably read somewhere that a 'probably right' and a smirk was the best way to try and turn the tables when getting dumped."

Erin thought some more.

"Yeah, you're…probably right."

We looked around the bar. The slim men drinking there were clearly tourists, Europeans probably. This bar must have been highlighted in *Condé Nast Traveler* or had a high ranking on TripAdvisor. I accidentally made eye contact with a lanky man with Bart Simpson-spiked hair so white only his white jeans were whiter. He took that as his cue to approach me.

"Shit!"

"What?"

"Here we go."

He approached us, a fruity drink in one hand and an iPad Air in the other. He spoke a language I couldn't identify into the tablet and then turned it toward me as it robotically spit out a translation:

"*You ladies want go back hotel with us?*"

He nodded back toward his friends who were smiling and bobbing their heads in unison toward us.

I didn't know whether to admire the man's aggressiveness

or be offended he might have thought we were escorts. He stood smiling a giant mouth of royal family horse teeth, waiting for my answer, holding out his iPad so I could offer my response. Before I had a chance to respond, Erin yanked the man's iPad from his hands and spoke firmly into it:

"Na, Ne, Non, Nein, Nicht, Nyet, Nej. No!"

She hit the translate button and returned the iPad to him.

"*No, no, no, no, no, no, no. NO!*"

He turned back toward his friends, confused. Erin slapped his little ass to get him on his way. I was impressed.

"So I guess I don't need to ask if you're back in the saddle again?"

"I'm...not sure. I think I'd like to be. Is it too soon?"

"It's not an offensive joke. It's never too soon, hon."

"Really?"

"Well...maybe for those Eurocreepers."

I laughed but she didn't join me.

Erin was currently in that self-absorbed place where she didn't actually care what I thought about anything. Even if she asked me a question tonight, she wouldn't really be asking what I thought, but instead asking in the hopes I would validate her already-determined decision: "What do you think, Cheryl, and if you think differently from me, I'll simply dismiss it."

I loved Erin, but when she was single she could be truly awful. Boys invaded her brain. In a relationship, even a not-so-great one, she was amazing. Relaxed, warm, and charming. My best friend. But single she was a woman with tunnel vision. A self-absorbed, myopic, man-hunter who'd float me up the Nile just to have some random stranger tell her she looked pretty.

Still, listening to Erin talk about dumping Joe was something I would tolerate all night if it meant I could get her back into a relationship ASAP. Unfortunately, she wasn't going to do it herself, she was terrible at choosing men, so tonight I would have to take the lead for her like I'd done so many times in her past.

"So...did you want to go talk to some other guys?"

Erin looked around the bar again.

"Not at this boozetrap, Cher..."

It wouldn't be easy, but the fact Erin was even willing to be out was a great start. Certainly better than us sitting in her apartment in our yoga pants eating ice cream all night. It seems strange that yoga pants are good for both intense workouts and intense gorging of fatty foods.

Erin's drink arrived and, as Sven handed it to her, he squeezed her upper forearm. At fancier spots bartenders seemed to think they had the right to do more than simply shake or stir our drinks.

"Then where should we go after that drink?"

I didn't believe Erin was truly into looking for a new man, she was just trying a coping method surely, but, still, the fact we'd be out and about, surrounded by available men, made me feel like I could make something happen. The more bars we went to, the more men we'd meet, the more potential lottery tickets there would be to scratch off and hope we'd find a prize and not just another stack of losers.

"Eh, you know I don't care about that stuff, Cher. Just pick some place...fun."

📍 **Belle Époque** (W. 58th St. and Eighth Ave.) | 6:01 PM

chapter three
SINGLE AT THE SAME TIME

So I picked Belle Époque, a bar designed to look like the interior of a swank French brothel. I'm not even sure Erin noticed, though, since she was so busy rambling on about her (and, unfortunately, *my*) dating life.

"But seriously, when was the last time we were single at the same time?"

I forced a smile at her.

"I mean, I know you've gone on some dates with that one guy. Whatever. The fact I haven't even met him tells me it's not that serious."

I nodded.

"You're a single girl for life, Cher. And I admire *that*." She put her hands on my knees. "You don't like to be tied down with your career and stuff. But, I *want* to be tied down."

"There are certainly worse fetishes."

Erin still wasn't listening to me.

"It's like…you wouldn't even know how to help me get back into a relationship."

"No, but maybe I could help you survive being single."

"What is there to possibly survive?!" Erin dramatically

threw her head back.

Erin had so rarely been a single women herself, and I'd so often been one. I'd added it up recently: 9,544 days single out of the 11,472 days in which I'd lived. During that time I'd learned…

"A lot."

"Well all I need to know is how to go from being a single woman to not being one. That's all I need!"

"I can teach you that."

I could teach Erin all the survival tips I'd learned from a life of singlehood. All this…*stuff* I'd thought about during those 9,544 days. All that stuff that had brought me to this point in my life.

"Cheryl, you're good at being a single woman, sure, and I love you for that, but you've never been great at *not* being one. No offense."

"None taken." I had no defense to that statement. "But, that's the reason why I can help you."

"Why?"

"Because I'm a woman who is actually happy with herself, no matter whether she is single. Or isn't."

"So?"

"So the world usually runs on the advice of angry women, not us happy ones. Think about it…"

"OK…"

"Who do girls first go to when they have boy troubles? They never go to me."

I was, for the most part, happy all the time. Single or coupled, winter or summer, in good health or bad, I was always happy, always smiling, always laughing. My advice was always positive, my glass always half-full, my viewpoint always optimistic. Yet my friends never went to someone like me for advice. No way. And I was tired of it.

"Who do they go to, Erin? Who do they get advice from?"

She didn't have an answer.

"They go to the angry women of the world. The bitter women. Those pissed-off, furious, frothing…bitches. Raging c-words. Even worse words if such words exist."

"Oh they do," Erin offered knowingly.

"And who do our particular friends go to for relationship advice?"

Erin thought about it for a sec before relenting.

"Amber."

"Yes. Amber. Or, more often than not, Amber comes to them. Forcibly."

Amber was a sorority sister of ours at Brown. She had grown up rich on the Upper East Side where she'd attended the city's finest private schools, had dined at its most famous restaurants, and, surely, literally owned several silver spoons. Rudy Giuliani had even attended her bat mitzvah!

But the problem was, Amber had never really known love. Her parents had a sham marriage. Her mother was a pill popper who slept with her riding instructor out in the North Fork. Her father was distant and lived most of the year down south on a golf course with a live-in mistress. And, while Amber's two sisters were stunningly gorgeous, Amber…wasn't so lucky. She sure tried her best, but a lifetime of thyroid issues made her frequently bloated, a series of rhinoplasties left her with a nose as thin as an asparagus stalk, and she could never quite control her acne.

So, despite all the material possessions in her life, money had not bought her happiness. Nor boyfriends. Yet she remained so worldly, so seemingly mature and intellectual, so *forceful*, that other women listened when she talked. And her talk was always centered around how terrible the male gender was:

"All men are cheaters!"

"You can't trust any of them!"

"They only care about one thing!"

Well of course she thought men were terrible. None of them would go out with her to try and acquire that "one thing"! A pity date here or there, usually only because her old man was important, a drunken hookup occasionally, but that was it.

So Amber took her anger out on other girls' relationships. Trashing guys, ripping on men, constantly trying to talk her so-called friends into dumping their boyfriends. But, my strategy was different. My strategy was actually the complete opposite. I meekly tried to convince Erin, *again*, to spend more time focusing on herself and less being angry at the world around her.

"Yeah, well, I don't see how even you can be happy right now. Cher, I thought I was done having nights like this. Amongst all these wasted losers. Total boozetrap. All these losers."

"You don't know they're losers."

"We're thirty-one years old. Didn't you think we'd be past this behavior by now?"

"I did. But that's not how it worked out. That's not how it was meant to be."

"I thought I would be with Joe forever."

"So did I."

"What went wrong with us?"

"Nothing. Maybe Joe just wasn't right for you."

"I didn't mean Joe and me *us*. I meant you and I *us*. What went wrong with us?"

"Nothing."

"Something must have."

Erin finished her drink in one big gulp and began fidgeting with her phone. She was not going to listen to my advice for the time being. I'd have to find another way to inject it into our night. Erin dropped her head down and punched something into her phone.

"How did we get here, Cher?"

"By a smelly cab ride."

"What?"

"Inside joke."

"With *whom*? I'm the only one here." Erin tossed her phone back into her purse. "I just texted Amber. She's going to meet up with us at the next spot."

I tried my best to hide my grimace as Erin turned, again putting her hands on my knees.

"Cher, what if we're actually the losers? What if we're the ones that don't know how to date? I don't want to go on more first dates again."

"The problem is we're always more worried about the first date than the last one."

Erin looked at me oddly.

"I have no idea what you're talking about."

"Look, a lot of people talk about first dates, worry about first dates, but eventually no one ever remembers them, right?"

"I guess."

"But you always remember your latest one. Your *last* one. I never told you about my last date with Trevor."

"Wait, what happened?"

I was finally ready to embarrass myself all for Erin's happiness. How was that for empowerment?

"Have you ever heard of *The Arabian Nights*?"

"I think."

"Well *The Arabian Nights* is the greatest story ever told. It's the story of this Persian king who kept selecting lucky towns-virgins to be his Queen for a night. This was a great honor—you had to be a beauty of the highest degree to be considered—but it was also a tragedy because, by the end of your one night of marriage, he would kill you."

"Kill you?"

"Yes! You see, Erin, after his brother's wife cheated on him, King Shahryar decided all women were unfaithful and that he should just kill them all before they ever had a chance to cheat on him."

"Good self-esteem there."

"That used to describe my dating life to a T. Often picked; always discarded. I usually lasted longer than a night, but not always. And only my self-esteem and dignity were killed, but still…"

With Trevor, I'd lasted nearly a year before he asked to end things. I hadn't seen him in a few days, our sex life had been floundering, and he wasn't answering my calls. I tracked him down in Midtown near the big bank he worked at.

"It wasn't, like, completely stalkerish because, like, I worked around there too. But it was kind of completely stalkerish because, like, I sat in the pavilion outside his office for a good three hours just staring at the revolving doors."

"You really did that?"

"Yes."

When Trevor finally spun through the doors at 7:07, he was surprised to see me, but probably not that surprised. Both because Trevor was a pretty cool customer, and because modern men have come to expect stalkerish behavior from the women in their lives. He quickly made up some lame excuse about having been busy at work, before admitting he no longer wanted to see me.

I was surprised at first but I shouldn't have been that surprised. This same thing had happened to me in the past with guys like Ollie and Gary and Ricky. Still, I started crying, which really freaked Trevor out. His coworkers began exiting the building and you could see him getting even more anxious.

"What happened?"

"He blurted out, 'Come on, Cheryl, what do you expect?' Which I realize, in retrospect, meant: 'How can you not expect us to break up when we no longer have any laughs, no longer have any sex, no longer love each other?' But, Erin, I took it to mean: 'What do you expect…to happen…like, *this* second?'"

"What did you do?"

"I blurted out the only thing I could think to blurt out: 'I expect one more date!'"

Erin giggled at my performance.

"I told him, 'You decided on our first date, now I get to decide on our last.'"

"Did that work?"

"Kinda. Trevor accepted a last date. Probably just so he could get away from a crazy lady yelling at him in the middle of 53rd Street."

"But still, you did it."

"Yes. I'd scored that last date. Now I just needed a plan. Let's go back to *The Arabian Nights*."

After marrying, sleeping with, and killing thousands of different women in the same amount of nights, King Shahryar pulled the name Scheherazade out of his Bingo hopper.

"Random name."

"Yeah. Scheherazade was a little different from all the previous wives too. She actually had a plan."

On the night of their marriage, once they retreated to the bedroom, but before they had sex, Scheherazade began telling the King a captivating tale of romance and intrigue. The King was totally sucked in. But, as the tale got right to its climax, Scheherazade yawned and ended the story on a cliffhanger.

This was quite the gamble, but Scheherazade was certain the King's curiosity would buy her another day of life. Indeed, it did. The King postponed her execution in order to hear the conclusion of her tale. But then, the very next night, guess what? Scheherazade again didn't just finish the previous tale but seamlessly began a new one which, of course, again ended on her yawning during an intense cliffhanger.

So it went for 1,001 nights, the King continually postponing her execution so he could see where her story was headed.

By the 1001st night, and she must have been running short on story ideas by then, the King finally decided he loved Scheherazade and would let her live forever.

"Erin, that was my plan too! I would set up an amazing last date with Trevor that would go on and on and on…"

"Until?"

"Until he was finally in love with me again."

chapter four
LAST DATE

Trevor met me at 7:00 in front of Petite Large as I had asked him to. He probably assumed this would just be another standard date like the fourteen others we'd had at "our" spot. I was certain it wouldn't be. I pulled up in front of the restaurant at 7:05 in the driver's seat of a 1979 Porsche 911 Speedster. He had been fooling around on his Blackberry, but looked up stunned.

"Where did you get this, Cher?!"

It was his dream car.

"Get. In."

I was trying to be cool and mysterious. I was in the driver's seat now, both literally and figuratively. My first stunt had worked, though it had set me back $500 for a four-hour rental from the Manhattan Classic Automobiles Club.

But I didn't tell Trevor that. I just pretended his purgatory girlfriend was a person who could make things happen. Exciting things. Things he'd love. Things he'd want in his life forever.

Trevor was itching to drive but I kept telling him, "In time." He was annoyed, but behaved himself, trying to convince me why he was so deserving of driving the Speedster that very moment. Perfect.

I zoomed through the Holland Tunnel and into New Jersey and, without giving anything away, navigated toward the Liberty State Park ferry dock. Trevor looked like he was about to cry as I handed the Porsche's keys to a valet, who whistled, shaking his head at just how lucky of a guy Trevor was.

"Don't worry, Trev', we'll come back to it."

"I want to drive it now—while there's still daylight!"

"My date. My rules. For the last time."

He nodded and, for a second, I lost my upper hand.

"Anyhow, by the time we get back to this car you're gonna get to do something better than just drive it."

"Fuck it?" he joked as we boarded a ferry and took off. "Where we going, anyway?"

"You'll see."

"Better not be Staten Island," he again joked. He was loosening up like he used to, cursing and joking and having fun. He was going along with my plan exactly, nicely playing into my hands. My plan, and the skipper's orders were to take a full lap around Manhattan island. This would take approximately two hours. I had to isolate Trevor from the rest of the world, from any other distractions. I wanted Trevor to feel like we were the only two people on the face of the earth.

I walked Trevor upstairs to the ferry's roof deck where we had a 360-degree view of the city and where a white linen table was set. I had looked up all the foods cultures throughout history considered aphrodisiacs and then, like the most crazy version of *Iron Chef* ever, had my chef for the evening prepare the meal:

*Avocado and asparagus salad (Trevor made a joke about stinky pee.)

*Oysters doused in horseradish (Trevor asked if they had washed ashore on Coney Island.)

*A certain animal's grilled penis (Trevor refused to eat it because it was "gay.")

I had rightly expected Trevor would want a beer, so I had my servers bring him a non-alcoholic one in a frosty mug.

When you want a date to last forever, or, at least until the person loves you again, the standard ingredient of most dates—alcohol—must be eliminated, I figured. Alcohol obviously makes dates more fun but it also speeds things up and generates a built-in end-game: passing out…or jumping into bed.

"It's fitting you served me this beer."

"Why?"

I was worried he had noticed it was non-alcoholic.

"Because it reminds me of sex on a boat…"

"Uh…?"

"Fuckin' close to water!" he cackled.

Paradoxically, sleeping together on this last date was *not* my goal. I would only use sex as a last resort. A "break in case of emergency" card.

After the big meal, after the decadent chocolate truffles had been served, I suggested we go to the middle deck for another surprise. As we descended the stairs, though, Trevor's mood seemed to change.

"Are you having a good time, hon?"

"I am. It's just…"

"Yes…?

Trevor touched his stomach and a queasy look came over his face.

Shit. I had totally forgotten Trevor always got seasick. I put my hand on his back, our first touch of the night, and he smiled warmly at me. Clearly a little seasickness wasn't going to ruin this night. Certainly a little seasickness wasn't going to end this last date—which now was looking more and more like the first date in the start of the second stage of our relationship. From last date to first date 2.0.

Music struck up from a live bossa nova band I'd hired.

You wouldn't expect it, but this square financial advisor, this former econ major from Vanderbilt, had a secret love affair with samba dancing. One night we had stumbled upon a Brazilian club on the Lower East Side and, tipsy on wine, had entered this samba dancing hot spot. We had the best time ever but by morning Trevor seemed a little embarrassed and I, admittedly, had to…well, admit, that samba dancing wasn't something I was likely to ever repeat. Trevor never brought it up again, though I was certain he secretly dreamt of a life where he removed his tie after a hard day's work and went samba-ing with his girlfriend until they'd sweated off five pounds each. Now here we were, again sweating and laughing as the band played "Mas Que Nada."

This last date was going better than I expected as our bodies rubbed close to each other in rhythm. I was starting to think by the time we got back to New Jersey, Trevor would surely be ready for the coup de grâce. The cargasm. An hour of racing the Porsche at 193 MPH around a lit track in Weehawken.

I'd intentionally set up these laps as a proxy for sex, as the climax of the night. But now I had to think we truly were going to have sex as our groins thrusted back and forth in samba motion. I wanted it bad! We hadn't had sex in weeks.

I'd thought we shouldn't have sex on this last date for strategic reasons. Like, maybe Trevor only agreed to go on one last date so he could sleep with me one last time. Guys were like that. But now I didn't care. Now I just wanted sex and I wanted Trevor and I wasn't worried about any stupid strategy.

I wasn't worried about the fact I'd plotted out and paid for a date that extended even after the cargasm with more food, more surprises, more fun. I simply wanted the captain to push down on the throttle and get the boat back to the dock as soon as he possibly could. I wanted to sprint to the cramped seats of the Porsche and make love to Trevor like we had back when we had first started dating.

I caressed Trevor's neck and he got goose bumps. We were still dancing in perfect rhythm. I was dancing better than I'd ever danced before. I felt Trevor's erection graze my inner thigh so, just as one song ended and before the next one struck up, I broke even more from my strategy and leaned in for a kiss. Our lips met for a millisecond before Trevor retracted and sprinted to the edge of the boat.

And there, Trevor began throwing up into the Hudson with a force I hadn't seen since freshman year sorority rush.

Shit!

I'd strategized for everything but seasickness. I'd thought of everything on this last date except bringing Dramamine.

I ran over to Trevor, now thinking that perhaps nursing him back to health was what would make him fall back in love with me. I now thought maybe some Florence Nightingale Syndrome was my best shot. I could live with that.

"Hon, you all right?"

"Can we…dock?"

"Yes, Trev, of course. I wish I'd thought of Dramamine. I'll go ask the captain. He'll surely have some."

Trevor wiped his face with the back of his blazer sleeve.

"I'm not seasick."

I took my hand off his back, confused.

"You're not?"

"I need to get off this boat."

"What is it? Are you not having fun?"

"Too much."

"Then…what?"

Trevor looked toward Manhattan.

"What is it, Trev…?"

"It's…"

He couldn't even look me in the eye.

"It's truly over, Cher."

Trevor wasn't in love with me any more. Trevor was now in love with Erika, a woman he'd met in a samba class he'd been taking secretly on nights I thought he was playing company softball. It now made sense why he never came home covered in dirt. I just assumed he rarely got on base. Wrong, he'd been hitting a lot of home runs actually.

Trevor had gone on this last date planning to let me down easily (and perhaps sleep with me) but he'd begun to have so much fun he began questioning his own feelings. But, the thing was, he was simply having fun, not falling back in love with me.

He was no more in love with me at any time during the date than he had been at the start of the date. No strategy in the world would make him love me again.

As he told me all that, I was sobbing my eyes out.

I had to figure out how to get off this boat.

I had to figure out how to get on with my life.

I had to figure out how I would possibly pay for $1847.38 of last date charges on my now maxed-out credit card.

I had to figure out how I was going to afford to feed myself for the next few months.

All I knew was, I still had two hours left on my Porsche rental and I was going to drive somewhere really fucking fast.

chapter five
COMMENT SENSE

"I drove 90 miles per hour all the way home to Rhode Island and spent the night at my parents' house. God, that was probably the dumbest thing I've ever done in my life and the last time I ever used strategy in my dating life."

Belle Époque had been a total flop and we'd felt like total hookers there.

"It was a good try though."

"No. My plan was about as bad as trying to make a serial-killing maniac king fall in love with you by telling, like, a *really* long story."

"All men have a little serial-killing maniac in them," Amber noted matter-of-factly. She'd met up with us on Broadway outside her office. She wore a brocade shell top from Erdem that probably cost more than my entire wardrobe, far too many bracelets on her wrist, and even more makeup.

"Where we headed, Cher? These shoes are killing me."

Amber was wearing some towering pumps from Tory Burch.

"We're just walking…"

We were just mindlessly walking down Broadway, the city

buzzing with excited people now off work and headed toward their first enjoyable act of the day if not week.

A homeless man slumped against a McDonald's, rattling a McFlurry cup of coins, called out to us: "Spare some change? Change into something more spare?!"

We cut a diagonal swath through Midtown, passing bodegas and diners, lumpy tourists lugging shopping bags from the M&M's store and Toys 'R' Us, middle Americans queuing up to get into the Carnegie Deli, preparing to see the new Patti LuPone show "Patti Cakes."

A construction worker doing road repairs with a jackhammer yelled out to us: "Yo, beautifuls. This ain't the only *JACK!-JACK!JACK!* large tool I'm licensed to operate." His buddy laughed.

We passed a restaurant called Appe-Thai-zing. A trio of businessmen dining al fresco intentionally talked loudly amongst themselves as we passed: "The little sluts always unleash themselves on Friday. TGFS."

I paid them no mind, instead wondering what was with all these Thai spots and their punny names. I quickly tried to name as many as I could: Thai-rific, Thai One On, Tant-Thai-lyzing, Thai-tanic?

A UPS man craned his neck at Amber's ass as he walked back. "Back that ass up. BEEP! BEEP! BEEP!"

Amber mumbled under her breath ("Pig."), but Erin exploded.

"What is going on?!"

"What?"

"Why is everyone making comments at us tonight?"

"It's no big deal."

She was still in a huff.

"It is a big deal, Cher."

"'How long have you lived in New York?"

"Huh?"

"You can't walk a block without getting commented on. You've never noticed this?"

Aaron Goldfarb | 25

"No!"

"It happens to me all the time."

"No it doesn't!"

"All the time. Hon, I once even kept track of all the comments made about me for an entire month."

"Really?"

"Graphed and charted."

"Why?" Amber looked confused.

"Uh, what can I say, I'm a nerd."

"You must have been really lonely."

"I thought I might make some project out of it."

"And…what did you find?"

Erin was flustered.

"Well…guys like to comment on my body."

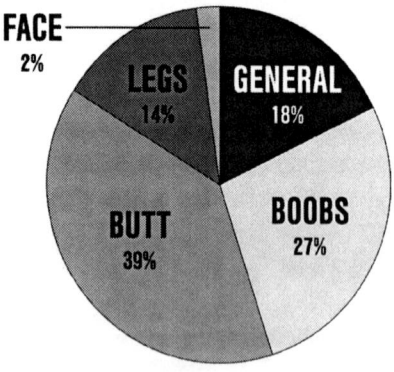

"Of course, Cheryl—you're gorgeous and have big boobs."

"I'm decent. And have a big butt."

"What else?"

"I bet you didn't know that any time of the day is a good

time of day for a little sexual harassment."

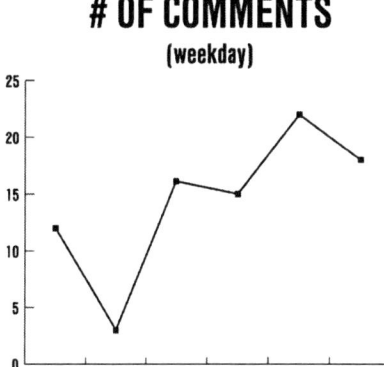

"OK…"

"And it's surprisingly the young men and the oldest men who are by far the biggest pervs."

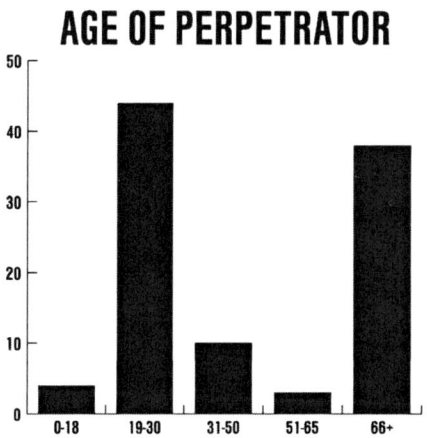

"That's kind of scary, Cher."

"It's *totally* scary, Erin," Amber noted. "Just another unfortunate byproduct of today's 'rape culture.'"

I didn't even know what that meant.

"Still. I get why you *get* comments, Cher. You're gorgeous. But me? I'm just…" She tailed off.

"Gorgeous too!"

"But I never get comments."

"Why would you want these New York street pigs objectifying you?!" Amber asked.

"Because…"

Erin didn't know how to say it, so I answered it any way.

"Honey, you and Joe didn't grow apart because of your looks."

"How can you be so sure?"

"Because I am. Seriously, start paying attention."

"To what?"

"To men on the street. Take your earbuds out and listen when you walk to work."

"And…?"

"And I bet you notice you get even more comments than me, that you get them more frequently, and I'd even bet they are far more lewd than anything I could ever possibly dream of getting!"

Erin was oddly touched.

"Really…?"

"Really."

"Fuck these men," Amber muttered. "You don't need any of them."

We passed a group of high-school-aged skate punks drinking 5-Hour Energy outside a CVS. One piped up, "MILFs I'd like to *fuuuuck*."

I elbowed Erin.

"See?!"

But Amber looked pissed, spinning back toward the boys.

"Why don't you stupid little virgins just shut up?!"

They immediately starting laughing at her.

"Come on…"

I grabbed Amber's wrist, pulling her back toward me and we kept walking. For once, Amber was now silent, embarrassed.

"Erin, you've just never had this comment sense before because you've never been single in this city."

"What's that gotta do with anything?"

"*Everything*. Single-ness gives us women a certain sixth sense. An amazing ability of observance and awareness." Then again, I thought to myself, sometimes women like Erin were single because they lacked self-awareness. "You'll see. The world will soon appear to you in a new X-rated light."

A street meat vendor made a lip-smacking, smoochy face at Erin.

"Hmmmm. Maybe I don't actually want that."

"It'll be fine."

I looked at Amber, now calmed down, she finally agreed with me. "It'll be…fine."

At the corner of 53rd, we came upon David Letterman's theater where a crowd of scummy-looking men were gathered outside, cameras slung around their necks.

"So what do you do now?"

"'*Do*?'"

"You said earlier you don't use strategy with men any more. Then what do you *do*?"

I smiled.

"I put my heart in the hands of fate."

"Fate?"

"Fate? That is so sappy, Cheryl."

Erin looked toward me. "But, really? Fate? I've always thought I should try to control everything."

"You can't, Erin. I've learned love is completely decided by fate. Neither party has a say in the matter."

"No one has a say in the matter," Amber noted.

"So how's that working out? Fate…?"

"Well…" I smiled, not sure if I was ready to reveal things. "It lead me to finally try online dating."

"No! You?!"

"I was so broke after that last date with Trevor I needed a way to scam some free meals!"

Erin genuinely laughed for the first time all night.

Eventually, Amber joined her.

"Speaking of, I'm starving."

"Me too, actually," Erin added.

"Have you not been eating since the break-up?"

Erin sheepishly nodded yes.

"Hon!" I gave her a motherly stare of disappointment.

"Sorry."

"It's OK. Because fate has actually brought us to a restaurant I've been wanting to try for awhile."

"Where?"

Just then the side door of the Ed Sullivan Theater opened and the gathered crowd of creeps exploded. Staring, gawking, shouting.

"This way gorgeous, give it to me, baby, give it to me!"

"Over here, baby, show me somethin'!"

"Gimme a smile, yeah, yeah, that's good! *Hot.*"

In a matter of seconds, the small crowd of a few dozen scummy men ballooned into hundreds of people from all walks of life. But Kim Kardashian just kept nonchalantly posing as everyone's cameras and smartphones and tablets took innumerable pictures of her, everyone likewise shouting innumerable comments at her, while she remained pretty much oblivious to everything being said around, and about her.

📍 **Twins** (w. 53rd St. and Broadway) | 6:34 PM

chapter six
TOGETHER ALONE

After we'd taken our own smartphone pics of Kim (obvi) and uploaded them to Instagram with a snarky hashtag (#kimyeah?) and comment ("Keepin' up?") added, I led Erin and Amber through the crowd and toward the restaurant right next door. It had a maroon awning with just the word **Twins** written on it in comic sans font, but its front windows were tinted too dark to see anything inside.

We headed through the brass double doors and into a mahogany foyer. The place seemed fairly bland, like a hotel restaurant in a boring convention city. But, I knew there had to be more. When I had first stumbled upon the restaurant's Yelp page, I must have laughed for a good half hour.

Twins - Midtown West, New York City, NY | Yelp
www.yelp.com/biz/twins-nyc
★★★☆☆ Rating: 3 - 123 reviews - Price Range: $$
1704 Broadway (corner of W. 53rd), New York, NY 10019 | Phone: (212) RU-TWINS
Description: Not just a silly gimmick (OK, maybe it is), this restaurant is owned and fully staffed by sets of twins.

We were greeted by the maitre d's, a thin man with slicked-back hair and a goatee…and, his identical twin brother. "Welcome to Twins! And what can we do for you *two*?"

The twin who spoke wore a nametag that read "Not Mitch"

while his brother wore one reading "Not Mike." Not Mitch kissed my hand while Not Mike kissed Erin's. Then they kiss-crossed.

"Dinner for three."

"How asymmetrical."

"But we can help."

The twin maitre d's led us into the bar area—staffed by two muscle-bound twins blending daiquiris—and sat us at a high-top.

"Cher...*look*!"

Literally every single employee of the restaurant, from servers to busboys, bartenders, and cooks were identical twins. Everywhere we looked, twins, twins, twins.

"So...?" I smiled. "What do you think?"

Erin looked around crazily. Amber looked perturbed.

"You know Betony is just around the corner?"

Just then, two spunky brunettes, Carol and Sharon, came to our table, speaking alternate lines.

"Hello, and welcome to Twins."

"The restaurant with the best *twin-ergy* around!"

"I'll pour y'all some H-*TWO*-Oh as you think about your drink orders."

"All drinks would have been 2-for-1 if either of you were twins."

"3-for-1 for triplets!"

"But for now, I might recommend our great scotch selection."

"All single malt. In fact..."

They now spoke together.

"It's the only *single* thing here!"

"Except for all us of course..." Erin mumbled toward me.

Carol and Sharon looked confused, so I quickly spoke up.

"Single malt sounds good. Doubles. For the three of us. Neat."

"Neato!" the twin-tresses simultaneously responded.

"Actually...I'll have a vodka soda," Amber told them. "Purity if you have it."

I warmly touched Erin's hand.

"You may be single now, honey, but you're not alone. We're together. All of us women. Now let's get you something to eat, you're skin and bones."

"Thanks."

I couldn't tell if Erin was thanking me for trying to cheer her up, or for "complimenting" her thinness. I didn't matter.

"I bet the food sucks here," Amber mumbled. "I mean, look at this menu."

She turned the photo-heavy laminated menu toward us. It was chock full of double cheeseburgers and twice-baked potatoes and triple-decker sandwiches.

"Have you ladies decided what you'd like?"

Carol and Sharon returned quickly with our single malts, setting massive double rocks glasses in front of us and a shaker pint of vodka soda in front of Amber. Amber took a strong suck of her drink and looked toward Carol and Sharon.

"So…?" she wondered. "How exactly does this work?"

"You tell us what you want, I go tell our chefs, and then we bring food to you in about fifteen minutes…?"

"No, not that." Amber scoffed. "I mean, I assume you have to be a twin to be hired."

"Exactly. Identically."

"But then what?"

Carol leaned in close to us like we were in a football huddle.

"Twins is owned by identical twin sisters, former Broadways understudies who never made it on the big stage. We are staffed entirely by forty-five sets of identical twins who work the same shift, in the same station, in the same uniform, on the same days."

"Did you have to come to the job interview together?" I wondered.

"Of course! Sharon and I had to create a dual resume even. If one twin calls out sick, the other one is sick too. If one twin gets fired, both twins gets fired."

"That's rough."

"It keeps us working hard. We'd never want to let each other down."

"That's nice…"

"Not only that, but look around. Everything is doubled. Double doors, double light fixtures, double bar stools. Guess what gum I'm chewing?"

"Doublemint!"

"Correct. As we like to say at Twins: this is the only place you'll be seeing double before you've had a drink!"

"You can only make a first impression once."

"But we make it twice!"

"So…what'll it be, ladies?"

Amber didn't even flinch before replying:

"I think we'll all share the Patty Fon-Duke."

"Our signature dish."

As Carol and Sharon walked away, we each took a sip of scotch. Erin winced and I gagged.

"I guess…we're not scotch drinkers?"

"Smoky. Smoky," was all Erin could spit out.

Amber smugly sipped from her vodka soda. Erin and I caught our breaths and drank some water just as Not Mitch and Not Mike led two nerdy-looking twins into the bar area, seating them across from two pretty female twins. Based on the awkward introductions it was clearly a blind date. I wondered if there were twin online dating sites. I nodded toward Erin and Amber and whispered: "Let's listen to this double date. Looks like double trouble."

"…John was born five minutes before me."

"That's OK, Ron. I like…younger men."

Erin whispered back.

"Those girls are *sexy*."

Amber shrugged.

"No, they're not. They're cute. Maybe even hot. But they're not sexy."

"What's the diff?"

"You see, Erin, I've determined you can either be sexy or lovable." Amber noted. "Or a bitch I guess."

"But what does 'lovable' even mean?"

I tried to take the floor from Erin.

"I've always thought lovable girls are the girl-next-door types. We wear our hair in ponytails and have pajamas that are pink and comfortable and warm. More akin to sweatsuits than lacy lingerie."

"I go with comfort when I sleep. So I'm 'lovable'?"

"Of course you are."

"Maybe not," Amber interjected again. "Because while cuteness is mainly a look, sexiness is mainly an attitude. Sexy girls can look like anything. They don't even have to be attractive. In fact, sometimes a girl is so sexy, you don't even realize she's of average looks until you closely examine her. Stupid guys love sexy girls."

"Yeah, you're right, Amber." Erin thought about it as Amber continued on.

"Sexy girls are who guys flock to in the bars. Single guys don't care about lovable girls and that's, for better or worse, what we are."

I looked at Amber. "Since when have you ever been 'lovable'?"

She laughed hard. "Never."

I loved being lovable though. I loved feeling big arms around me in a bear hug. I loved getting kissed lightly on the lips. "Just 'cause I love you." Having my hand held as he walked me down the street. Spooning with him in bed and him making me feel warm. Rubbing my shoulders and feet and head. Letting me snuggle under a blanket with him while we watched TV on the couch.

"I love being lovable and I love when a man's lovable to me. Unfortunately, Erin, I've learned you can never attain the lovable without being sexy. You're only gonna get a man to be lovable to you if you first reel him in by being sexy."

"So you're saying I have to be sexy to meet another man?"

"You must!"

"Don't bother," Amber exhaled.

"But how?"

"By being coy and mysterious. Wearing your Hanky Pankys instead of those comfy cotton briefs. Hanes Her Way? No way. Sleeping naked with him even though you're freezing your butt off. Letting him kiss you deeply and fuck you aggressively. You taking charge and going down on him. Climbing up and getting on top of him. Rocking his freaking world!"

Erin looked timid while Amber looked surprised.

"That's not natural. For me."

"Me neither!"

Erin thought of something.

"Hey, wait a sec. You said to stop having strategies and just let the fates handle things."

"But Erin, that's the thing…sexiness *isn't* a strategy. When you meet the right man, you'll naturally become sexy for him. Because that's how he'll make you feel."

I glanced over at the double blind date once more. The women were clearly not interested in the men and that's probably why they weren't being sexy. Why they weren't twirling their hair and being flirtatious. Why they were just *being*.

Carol and Sharon brought over a cast iron pot of steaming gruyère and some crudités.

"Do you mind if we also bring the bill? It's the end of our shift…"

Even though I hated when servers did that I nodded and they walked off to their POS system to prepare our bill. Erin subtly nodded toward them.

"I wonder if they secretly hate this? Like, do they go back into the kitchen and just think about killing themselves?"

"Double-barreled shotgun?"

"Three lame puns and you're out."

"Fine. But I seriously hope you didn't find this place too… *cheesy*."

I took a baby pickle and dunked it into the fondue. Delicious.

"I find your puns cheesy."

"Good."

Erin laughed. It was working. Even Amber seemed to be having a good time. I nodded toward our glasses.

"Let's try again."

We took another sip of our scotches. They went down slightly better on a second attempt. A metaphor for our dating lives perhaps.

"Cheesy or not, thank you, Cher. I was really down in the dumps when we entered here. But now? Now I'm on cloud nine."

"No, you're on cloud two."

"That's three!"

I shrugged. "Cloud 2 would make a good name for a bar."

Erin laughed. "You and your ideas."

"One day."

Amber rolled her eyes.

"OK, we have to move to a new spot, ladies. This double-ness is making you two delirious."

Amber threw some crisp twenties into the leather-bound bill folder.

"What? You don't have any two-dollar bills?"

"You guys really need to find a man tonight. And, actually, so do I…" Amber stood.

We headed for the exit. As we passed Not Mitch and Not Mike, one of them spoke up out of the side of his mouth to Erin and I, like a drug dealer in Washington Square Park.

"You two ever 'mirror-imaged'?"

I stopped short, not sure if I'd heard him correctly.

"Um…excuse me?"

Just then the Not Mitch and Not Mike both rhythmically thrust their hips back and forth, mimicking having sex with Erin and me. Indeed, it did look like a mirror image, though less erotic and more like a Marx Brothers routine. Amber was disgusted, but Erin was laughing so hard I had no choice but to join her as we exited out the double doors.

"What freaks!"

We stood back out on Broadway, the *twin-ergy* slowly leaving our systems as we headed west toward Hell's Kitchen and the next random stop on our evening's journey.

"I need to get a new boyfriend ASAP so I can take him back there."

"Yeah, right. With all the other great restaurants in this city to take a date?"

"Oooh, Restaurant Week is next week. We should hit a hot spot, guys."

"Oh my God, did I ever tell you about this crazy couple I met?"

chapter seven
RESTAURANT WEAK

So apparently Tripp discovered NY Magazine's list of the Top 101 New York City restaurants and became determined to conquer them all. Every Friday night (ideally at 8:00), Saturday night (ideally at 9:00), and late Sunday afternoon (ideally at 5:00) he booked a reservation at a top-ranked spot.

Sometimes these reservations had to be scored more than a month in advance using very complicated methodologies, while others were first-come, first-serve. Tripp meticulously kept track of his dining schedule in iCal, which he shared with his assistant who did most of the bookings. Tripp figured, in thirty-four weeks, he and his wife Tori could knock off all 101 restaurants.

One Friday back in January, Tripp had a 9:15 reservation at Gramercy Tavern, a place he was embarrassed he hadn't already been to. He thought a man in his position in life should have dined there years ago and already found it passé by now. He should have seen it as a place merely to take out-of-town clients he and his coworkers thought to be rubes.

Tripp and Tori walked in at 8:50 and the service captain coolly informed them their table wasn't yet ready. They moved to the bar (which was also, fancily enough, reservation only) and where they were forced to stand. They each had a $14 cocktail that took the vested bartender eight minutes to make. Tripp ordered a Sloe Storm, not exactly sure what sloe gin was. He enjoyed the non-boozy sweetness of the drink as he still wasn't fully able to enjoy stiffer classics like Manhattans, Old Fashioneds, and Sazeracs. Tori selected an Orange Blossom made with elderflower, a refreshing cordial she always ordered when she saw it listed as an ingredient in fancy specialty drinks.

Their conversation while hovering at the lively 17th-century-esque bar focused on the lavish floral displays around the restaurant. Tori noted how remarkable it was all this greenery was actually inside the high-ceilinged restaurant as if it were some botanical garden. Tripp, well-researched on each Top 101 restaurant they dined at, had read that very morning, on his downtown commute to the Financial District, that Gramercy Tavern amazingly employed a full-time florist. The woman set up new displays each week according to the seasons and holidays for a salary of around $100,000 a year. Tripp also discussed how—due to the on-going recession—his Q2 bonus was looking like it would only be around $75,000. Tori wondered if they would have to alter their Mediterranean vacation plans. She shuddered at the thought of having to stay at a…Marriott.

Meanwhile, just about fifteen blocks to the south and east, two other people, let's call them David and Casey, sat at a hot dog joint they'd stumbled upon while strolling on St. Mark's Place. For just twelve bucks they'd gotten two hot dogs (he, one bacon-wrapped and slathered in a special house dressing; her, a tofu dog topped with fresh vegetables and spicy jalapeños), a side of cheesy tater tots they shared, and a can of PBR each.

This was only their first week dating and between greasy bites they discussed David's struggles to get funding for his startup and Casey's struggles to get any of her freelance work sold. She and David had already had sex five times that week and would have sex four more times that very weekend.

If you counted backwards to the last time Tripp and Tori

had had five to nine instances of sex, the fifth most recent act would time travel you back to July of the previous calendar year, while the ninth would put you at his birthday in mid-March. Tripp looked over at Tori who fondled the stem of her wine glass. She was now on her third drink of the evening—having switched to a dry riesling from the Finger Lakes. She noted that she found it rubbery in taste. They hadn't even been served their main courses yet, and since Tripp had mentioned his Q2 bonus woes the conversation had not diverted from anything besides meta-discussion of the actual restaurant they currently sat in. Tripp was impressed by the dining room's staid atmosphere, upscale clientele, and service, though Tori thought Minetta Tavern (#14 on the Top 101) had much better food and drink if she were to quibble. Tripp thought he could probably have sex with Tori that night. He didn't really want to though. He was far more interested in his duck breast confit, which NY Mag had called a "can't miss" item. Tripp always ordered the "can't miss" item.

David and Casey looked around the 150-square-foot hot dog joint with a fire marshall capacity of twelve and quietly had a few laughs at the other skeevy diners surrounding them. In seats to their right, some wasted NYU kids shoved corn dogs drenched in yellow mustard into each other's faces. During the rare moments their mouths were empty they discussed their sex lives in intimate detail. It seemed like each and every combination and permutation of couples, threesomes, and so on (amongst the five coeds) had actually occured. Casey surely wasn't a prude, but the conversation made her blush. At the front counter sat two crusty longshoremen types, though nowadays they could have easily just been ironic East Village hipsters. In the corner, under a Schlitz sign, a punk couple made out, blocking the mustard pump from any would-be pumpers, as the two stuck their pierced tongues deep down each other's throats. Casey thought it was a perfect setting for a perfect date.

Tripp was greatly enjoying his meal at Gramercy Tavern. He had thought the first course of beef carpaccio had been exquisite. He likewise found the duck breast confit to be sublime. It had come, chef's recommendation (Tripp always followed chef's recommendation, which annoyed Tori), rare. The meat was a gorgeous, tender pink and folded into the greens and shiitake mushrooms. Service had been immaculate and Tripp would eventually tip 17.5% on the $262 check. Tori wasn't sure the restaurant deserved a spot on the Top 101 as she hadn't been completely wowed. She thought #95 Waverly Inn had a cooler crowd, #34 The Porter House better marbleized cuts of meat, #5 Craft superior cocktails, and #3 Per se a far more adventurous dining experience (though sitting across the table from Tripp for nearly four hours had been excruciating). Tori mainly wished, though, that Tripp would hurry up and throw down his glass of tawny port (ever since his last promotion he'd taken to ordering dessert wines to end meals) so they could get home. She just wanted to be alone to watch the last three weeks' Million Dollar Listing New York saved on the DVR while Tripp slept off his sixty-hour work week.

David and Casey strolled up Park Avenue holding hands, headed to her East 29th Street apartment, a converted one-bedroom she shared with a rotating stream of struggling actor buddies. They had grabbed cans of Sixpoint from a corner bodega and decided to enjoy a moonlight mile-long walk home while drinking them right out of the brown bags. This was much better than a packed bar, they tried to convince each other, though neither needed convincing. She truly knew it was better. En route to Murray Hill, David pointed out great restaurants they passed, which he claimed he would take her to in a few months when he was certain he would have a little more time and money.

"You really haven't been to Momofuku? Their ramen is amazing. Although...who really cares all too much about fuckin' noodles?" "That's Casa Mono. You can sit at the bar and watch them cook your meat!" "ABC Kitchen is down that street. Obama has fundraisers there!"

Casey found it endearing he wanted to one day treat her

to these nice restaurants even though they'd just begun dating. But, she didn't really care. She'd gone to plenty of "nice" restaurants when she was much younger and dating much older men. Now, though, as long as she got to spend time with David, she would have been perfectly happy to simply go to Shake Shack every night.

Exiting Gramercy Tavern, Tripp and Tori were already on to anticipating Saturday and Sunday's Top 101 meals: Babbo and Eleven Madison Park. Tori loved Batali—even though it was no longer "cool" to—and was psyched they'd actually gotten a res (you had to call Babbo's reservation line at 10 AM exactly one month before the day you wanted to dine there). Tripp was thrilled to finally get to try NY Mag's #1 overall restaurant in Eleven Madison Park.

"Look, Case'! Gramercy Tavern. Still Danny Meyer's best and probably Manhattan's most famous restaurant."

"Who is Danny Meyer?" asked Casey, curious. She liked food, she just didn't "know" food.

David wasn't annoyed Casey knew nothing about New York dining. Her lack of pretension made her far more alluring. He grabbed her hand and pulled her in tight to keep her warm as snow began to fall.

"You probably know him best as the guy behind Shake Shack."

"Great burgers." She smiled.

"Yeah."

Tori put her hand up to hail a cab and get them out of the impending snowstorm, but Tripp immediately swatted it down. It was the only time he had touched Tori all evening. Tori scoffed at the thought her husband would make $580,000 that year, even with a subpar Q2 bonus, and spend nearly a grand on meals that very weekend (after $262 at Gramercy Tavern, $175 at Babbo, and a whopping $195/person on Eleven Madison's tasting menu before they'd even added the sommelier-recommended wine pairings), yet he couldn't splurge $12 for a cab ride back to the Upper West Side?!

"One day I'll take you, Case', I promise."

"I know you will, D. In fact, maybe one day…that'll be us."

Casey nodded toward Tripp and Tori, just as they were about to step into a slowing cab Tori had decided to spend her "own" money on. She noticed both Tripp and Tori were dressed to the nines, he in a Hugo Boss suit, she in a Kate Spade dress, looking so handsome and pretty and rich and successful and happy and…New York.

"Well I sure hope not."

David laughed hard before he kissed Casey deeply. She tasted tater tots and cheap beer on his breath. She thought it was the best taste in the entire world.

📍 **Drunx Pub** (w. 53rd St. and Broadway) | 7:50 PM

chapter eight
SEARCHING FOR THE CLICHÉ

"Cheryl, you know where I want to go now?"

"Where?"

"One of those bars we used to go to back when we were young."

"Back then we were pretty stupid too."

"OK. Then I want to go to one of those bars we used to go to back when we were young *and* stupid."

"But why?"

"Because I want to meet someone younger and stupider than me."

"I'm not sure Em will like that."

"Who cares! You know she'll only hang with us for a drink or two anyway."

At the corner of 53rd and Ninth we saw Emily standing under a pizzeria awning quickly tapping her high-heeled foot on the sidewalk as she futzed around on her iPhone. She looked up at the three of us.

"Looks like it's been a *real* happy hour for you three." We laughed. "Apparently, I need to catch up. Where we going?"

"How 'bout…Drunx?" I offered.

"What is *that*?" Danielle wondered.

"I'm not sure. But a friend recommended it. Come on."

And so I marched us toward Drunx, a dive on Eleventh I'd never been to but which, based on a friend's recommendation, sounded like the perfect place to continue Erin's evening of distraction. And, an even more perfect place to piss off Emily, who huffed and puffed as we continued heading west.

"Before you know it, we'll be in *Jersey*."

At the entrance to Drunx, the bouncer held up his beefy forearm like a tollbooth barricade, preventing a short-forming line of people from entering.

"*Ah-dees*, ladies."

"Seriously?" Emily asked.

"Seriously." He responded.

"What is this, a Chili's?" Emily exclaimed, handing her NYS driver's license over.

Being asked for an ID is usually something that makes a woman of our, *ahem*, age feel good about herself, but not Emily. In fact, Emily still looked like a sorority girl, which was something that had served her well in both her life and career.

"Is something wrong?!"

As the stereotypically massive bouncer scrutinized her driver's license, Emily saw fit to take offense to this most typical of nightlife acts. And, when the Hulk put her license into a handheld scanning device to prove its legitimacy, Emily saw fit to snap in her stereotypically snotty way.

"Is this…1999 or something? Because that's the last time I used a fake."

The bouncer, clearly used to snotty little Manhattan girls who tried to snot their way to getting their way, was not fazed.

"You have a second form of photo ID, Miss?"

That was not the way to get Emily's cooler head to prevail, not that any one ever saw her cooler head.

"A second form of photo ID?! Who the fuck carries a second form of photo ID?! What would *that* even be exactly?!"

"You know, a passport, office ID, *liberry* card…"

"Who goes to the library?! I got a thousand books on my fucking phone!"

Emily pulled out her iPhone and began furiously punching something into the screen with such a force I was certain her freshly manicured fingers were going to shatter the glass. In the meantime, Amber, Erin, and I gave the bouncer our IDs, which he barely glanced at before accepting them as legit.

"Well, Miss, if you don't got that second form of ID, I'm gonna have to ask you to step out the line."

Emily turned her iPhone around, lifted her arm straight up in the air so the screen was at the bouncer's eye level, just inches from his eyes, and showed him what was on it.

Emily Silver

From Wikipedia, the free encyclopedia

Emily Miriam Silver (born July 3, 1980[1][2]) is an American actress, model, and reality television personality most famous for her supporting work in the movies The Vise (2008) and The Honey Trap (2009) and being in the cast of season one of reality show Manhunters (2012). She has had several noteworthy relationships with male celebrities, most notably Mark Ruffalo and Chris Hardwick[3].

"Will my fucking Wikipedia page work?!"

The bouncer calmed perused the modest entry, commenting to himself as he noticed certain "highlights."

"Both your license and Wikipedia say you're 5'4", 110 pounds…"

He smiled, letting the fact linger in the dense Hell's Kitchen air. Emily was 5'2" and more like 120 pounds. Of course, she was also vain enough to lie on her DMV application and have her personal assistant Meghan constantly tweak her Wikipedia page to make it as flattering as possible. Likewise, Emily had once had a three-minute conversation with Mark Ruffalo at a party, which Meghan had somehow turned into one of the first three lines of her official bio.

"So…?"

The bouncer threw his head backwards toward the front door: "Go in."

As we entered, I heard him cackling heartily.

"Do you believe that asshole, Cher? What a power trip. Overgrown pituitary case. At least my job isn't written on my shirt. Did you see what he was wearing?! 'STAFF.' It just said 'STAFF' in all caps on his stupid quadruple X tee."

"OK, settle down, hon. Let's enjoy our night."

"I will. As soon as I get a fuckin' drink."

Drunx was energized and sweaty. After-work Fridays in Manhattan always are, especially at bars that attract a young clientele happy to cram into a tight space. These were people simply excited their work weeks were over at their miserable jobs they assumed they would only have for a short time, until they aged their way up to something more interesting or lucrative. Of course, I sadly knew, they would soon find out that wouldn't be the case. And, by the time they got to my age, they'd be so beaten down they wouldn't even go out on Friday nights with the same reckless zeal any more. In fact, like me, they might barely go out at all.

"Check out that tool with the box on the bar. He must have just been fired." Emily laughed.

Meanwhile, Amber's head was on a swivel, examining all the men in the joint. "Where?"

"Over there—"

I turned toward the bar and then I saw him. No, not the "tool," if he indeed was one. *Next* to the tool.

Next to the tool sat the most handsome man I'd ever seen. You could have called it love at first sight but that wasn't quite accurate. It was a sighting, and he was certainly a sight, but I'm not sure I could cite it as love. I wondered why my handsome man was talking to this tool, and what was indeed in the tool's box. I hoped to find out eventually.

We moved to the corner and took seats near an open window, the last streaks of the sunset coming over the Hudson and into the dark bar. Erin and I ordered mugs of beer from a tatted-up waitress, Amber stuck with a vodka soda, while Emily tried to get a white wine spritzer, which was quickly denied her. She begrudgingly switched to a Hendricks and tonic "with a twist" (she always tried to sound like a movie character when ordering drinks.)

"Why are we at this dump, Cher?"

"To meet men. For Erin."

"Me too!" Amber noted.

Erin feigned shock. "Come on. You make me sound pathetic."

Emily wasn't amused. We were well in sight of the bouncer, who now let everyone in without checking anything more than the women's asses as they sauntered by.

"Why would Erin want to meet a man here? He would be the kind of man who would be…*here*."

"I was thinking the same thing," Amber added.

Emily continued looking around, disgusted, before she noticed something.

"That one guy next to the toolbox isn't that bad. Don't look! Ooh, he stared over here for a sec. Do you think he recognized me? Hmmm…I hope so, because other than him…this place is total ass."

Erin was getting annoyed. She had less tolerance for Emily than I did.

"We know. That's what we want."

"This ass bar is what you want?"

"Yeah, I want an ass bar to get some ass at."

Emily still didn't get it. A couple of entering bar patrons stared at her as the waitress returned with our round.

"Really?" Emily was stunned. Erin leaned toward her ear, the exasperated wind from Erin's breath causing Emily's diamond earrings to swing like porch chimes.

"Really, because I want to find a young guy here that will

fuck me so good I forget all about Joe."

"Oh."

Erin leaned back, pleased with herself for rendering Emily speechless. But only momentarily.

"But how could you not have already forgotten about Joe? He was so…forgettable. I can already barely remember what he looked like. Not to mention, no young guys can fuck worth a shit."

Erin was about to dive from her barstool and knock Emily off her seat, but Amber restrained her. Emily hadn't even noticed as she continued surveying the scene. A scene she had been making a scene in, which other patrons had begun to notice. A guy a few feet away tried to surreptitiously take a long-distance selfie of him with Emily in the background.

"But seriously…? This place does suck. If you're really interested, there's a party tonight for some new Swedish facial gel. I can't even pronounce it. Weird letters like that "o" with the line through it. Their publicist told me to bring as many camera-friendly girl friends as I want."

"Nah, I don't think so," I muttered.

"You'll get gift bags with their full line of products. Expensive stuff."

"Yeah, we don't think so," pitched in Erin.

"But no one else in America has these products yet!"

"It sounds fun, Em, but not tonight. We're just gonna stay here in Hell's Kitchen. Bar crawl around this 'hood all night."

"They're made with exfoliants from the Baltic Sea!" Emily pleaded.

"It sounds…lame," Erin noted.

"Lame?!" Emily stood, becoming animated. Some drunk dudes watched, soaking it all in. "It's gonna be stocked with some of the hottest young actors around. Not childish, drunk, $30k-a-year junior paralegals like here!"

That line made the guys laugh pretty hard, though Emily didn't even notice. One of the guys saw an opportunity and came over.

"Uh…can I get a pic?"

Emily quickly calmed down and smiled wide. "Of course."

The guy held his Droid out at arm's length, put his arm snuggly around Emily in a way she'd never allow a random non-celebrity to do unless there was a camera nearby, and snapped a pic.

"I loved you in…*that thing*."

"Thanks."

The guy quickly glanced to make sure the picture was to his liking, held his arms in the air and "Woohooed!," and returned to his buddies, who gave him a round of high-fives. That would be a mobile upload with snarky commentary within seconds.

"Come on Cher, it's gonna be fun. The Kardashians are supposed to be there. My agent might even introduce me to Kendall."

I looked at Erin and we both tried not to laugh. Emily was rarely celebrity-spotted herself any more, especially in neighborhoods like Hell's Kitchen as opposed to the touristier spots full of middle Americans who probably thought her glamorous, but when she actually was spotted she rarely acted surprised.

It was always hard to tell whether people wanted a pic with her because they were starstruck or because they were struck with an opportunity to mock a C-list (or whatever she was) celebrity. At least she was pretty, so it didn't matter to most guys. Her minor celebrity just gave them an icebreaker to talk to her. I would have hated this, but she ate it up. It was a kind of disease. One with no antidote except becoming more famous.

"I don't particularly consider hanging out with skinny little actors who can't drink fun," I noted.

"How can you not?!" Emily was getting apoplectic. "They're all so…gorgeous."

"And so very…straight."

"They could also be rich and famous soon. You have to prospect.

"Maybe that's what we're doing with the, what'd you say?, 'young, drunk, $30k-a-year junior paralegals' here."

Aaron Goldfarb | 51

"Cher, prospecting here is like a gold miner going to the desert!"

Erin hadn't spoke for awhile, but that didn't mean she'd given up on the argument.

"Emily, you're such a cliché."

"A cliché?"

It was like a punch in the face, yet an odd calmness came over Emily.

"Yes."

"I'm a cliché?!"

"That's what I said."

Emily laughed histrionically.

"Erin, you're the cliché."

"How am I a cliché?"

"Looking for a drunk young idiot to fuck the misery from you."

"And…?"

"And eventually you'll meet another man and he'll be a cliché too. Raised around here, probably Jewish, certainly in finance. He might have been interesting in college but by now he'll be as bland as his friends. He'll become your finance fiancé! You'll get married in a cliché ceremony, move to a cliché town in the New York or New Jersey suburbs and soon you'll have boring cliché kids who will grow up to also search for the cliché love they've seen on cliché TV shows!"

"Like the one you starred in?"

Emily nodded, but she wasn't mad. "*Exactly*." She looked Erin in the eye and warmly touched her shoulder. "What I'm saying is: you're so smart and pretty Erin. You don't have to be a cliché."

Erin smiled and Emily must have thought she had finally gotten through to her.

"I *want* that cliché, Em. So does Cheryl."

"Amber doesn't," Emily noted.

Amber shook her head, begrudgingly and spoke meekly. "I do."

"99.9% of women do. That's why it *is* a cliché. Because we all want it." Now, Erin put her hand on Emily's shoulder. "I'm only sorry you don't."

Emily put her hands into the middle of the table, touching all our forearms.

"Maybe one day I will. But not today, unfortunately." She grabbed her Jimmy Choo clutch. "I love you guys, I really do. I know we don't agree on a lot any more, but I couldn't live without you all." She quickly sucked down the rest of her G&T. "So…good luck living a cliché night and finding that cliché guy. Me? Well, I'm going to go try to get written about in the gossip pages."

She kissed us all on the cheeks, and left.

"I've never seen her so brutally honest."

Erin looked at me. "Yeah. And don't tell her, but she was actually kind of right. The guys here are totally miserable."

"Yeah…"

Just then a dorky businessman came over to our table, looking a little confused.

"The bouncer is telling everyone Em from *Manhunters* is here. Is that true?!"

"I think it was just someone who looked like her."

The dork looked bummed out.

"Damn! She's like…my dream woman!"

I looked at Erin and Amber as the man walked away. "To think…he could have been The One."

"Yeah, but what does that even mean any more?!"

chapter nine
THE HIERARCHY OF THE ONE

Brooklyn College is just three miles away from where we currently drink. There in 1943, in his paper "A Theory of Human Motivation," a psychology professor named Abraham Maslow came up with a theory called the hierarchy of human needs. Which, of course, he put in pyramid form.

For a while there, from Giza to the food groups, everything was in pyramid form. It was a very popular shape until the carb-less crowd came along and everyone realized we didn't need seven servings of bread a day. But, back in the '40s, pyramids were still cool and Maslow's pyramid was the coolest.

The base of his pyramid was built on physiological needs. Drinking water and breathing air, eating food and eliminating it, sleeping and sleeping together. Next up was safety and health. Security of you and your family. Gainful employment. As the pyramid got smaller, needs became less important. In the middle was love and friendship. A sense of belonging. Self-esteem. Confidence, achievement, respect from others. And, all the way at the tip top of the pyramid, you had actualization as a human being. Most people don't even know what that term means, then or now. Probably why so few people are actually actualized.

Now, lots of women talk of finding "The One," but we only seem to have a foggy feeling about what that might entail. That's silly! Surely all us women want similar things out of our The One, even if we might not necessarily be able to find those men with those rare things way up at the tip top of the pyramid.

The base of the pyramid of the Hierarchy of The One is: money. Wealth. Don't deny it, Erin, it's true. It's what matters most. In fact, it might be *all* that matters. But it's not quite why you think. Many women will say money doesn't matter to us. Always to "us." But, it does. So, so much it does.

I'm not saying all women are gold-diggers. Certainly not. I'm not and you know that. But what I am saying is: all women are stability-diggers. We all need men that earn money. Or *will* earn money. Even if we earn plenty, we still want a man, The One man that will be our man forever, to have money. If not now, soon. Damn soon. I'm not sure why, but this probably goes back to our Paleolithic ancestry where The CaveOne had to be the kind of man who was a solid hunter. The CaveOne's hierarchy:

APPRECIATION
FOR QUALITY CAVE ART
HAS A FEW TEETH
DOESN'T SMELL TOO BAD
ABILITY TO HUNT TASTY ANIMALS
LIFE EXPECTANCY OVER 23 YEARS

The next level on our hierarchy of The One is simply not *being* gross. You say, don't you mean being attractive? No. Good-looking? Nope. Decent-looking? Not even. A man, to be The One, simply has to not be gross. Us women can quickly talk ourselves into falling for a man if he is simply *not* gross. Like, he just needs to be above 5'6" and under 350 pounds and occasionally shower and sometimes shave. He just needs to be a 2 out of 10 on that crude scale guys use to talk about us women when they're out drinking together.

I've been stunned how ugly some of the men are that our friends have fallen in love with. Jeez, I could say the same about myself if I went back and looked at old pictures of old crushes. But, so long as that wealth and stability base is there, we really don't care if he's bald or chubby or has moobs instead of pecs. Silly boys think we care. That's why they do so many push-ups.

Don't get me wrong, we'll be *way* interested if he looks like Tom Brady or Matt Damon. But if he's poor, unstable, and unsuccessful, we'd never have much long-term interest in him. Though, we'd probably make out with him once or twice, preferably in public so our friends would see.

Next in the hierarchy, the third level, the middle, is that The One has to love us. Being so madly in love with us—and frequently reminding us of that—is more important than most men realize. I've seen so many of my friends fall for a guy simply because he was madly in love with her. Not creepy, stalker love. Not lust either (though, that is nice), but a pure expression of love. The little things: holding hands in public, buying occasional roses, hanging out with our friends and pretending to actually enjoy that.

So tonight, Erin, if I was teaching a guy how to go from being just another someone to being your The One, I'd tell him to be stable and bland, a little rich and a lot predictable, to be showered…and shower you with love. Those are the prerequisites for being The One. Everything else is gravy. "Extra credit" we might pray our The One also has. Yet, it's these top two tiers of the hierarchy that guys strive so hard to attain above everything else. Like a good personality.

Can you believe that? Personality goes a long way, right? Wrong. It hardly matters. Being smart and interesting, funny and fun, it matters for a first date. But, it hardly matters for the long haul for being The One.

Don't believe me? Then ask yourself this: when you meet

married women's husbands, do you ever find them entertaining? At dinner parties, do you aim to plant yourself next to the married men and watch them hold court? Of course not. Because they can't hold court. They can only hold their wives' giant purses.

Married men are boring. Now you probably assume they got boring *after* they got married. That their wives stripped their personality from them. You'd be wrong. They were always boring. Always vanilla and uninteresting. That's why they are married.

A lack of personality you see is synonymous with stability. The exciting guys may get more ass than a park bench, but they never become The One. Because that's the thing: as we get to the top of the pyramid we see traits that help men get laid, but don't help them get relationships.

Stuff like being legitimately attractive and incredibly good in bed. Having a six-pack and a big dick. Riding a motorcycle and being good at basketball. Totally irrelevant to being The One!

Guys with big dicks are usually…big dicks. They're bad in bed 'cause they're selfish in bed. They're selfish in bed because they're selfish in life. Because they're handsome and have always gotten their way. They didn't have to become smart or educated or interesting or funny. They've never cared about having a good job or solid stability. They didn't need it and they still don't need to have it. And they're never the type of guys you want to spend the rest of your life with.

But, as I said, they can still be fun to mess around with for a night.

📍 **Duane Reade** (w. 50th St. and Broadway) | 9:03 PM

chapter ten
2014 BC

"So are you telling us you're looking to hook up tonight, Cher?"

"You never know."

I smiled.

"Well you look good."

"Yeah, I like that sweater, Cher."

"Oh God, I've had it forever."

"It's cute. Where'd you get it?"

"Come to think of it, Gary got it for me."

I touched the lilac cashmere, it was still so soft.

"Ew, Gary." Amber cringed. "He was so gross. I'd think you'd want to burn that."

"It's expensive."

"Who cares?" Erin added. "I trash everything that reminds me of exes."

"Really?"

"Trash it, set it on fire, throw it into a dumpster, sell it on eBay, donate it to charity. Goodwill can have everything I own from men I now have nothing but ill will toward. The Salvation Army can take everything that reminds me of relationships I couldn't salvage."

"If I did that—I might not own a thing!"

"You're the only girl I know who hates clothes."

"I don't hate clothes. I hate shopping."

"Same thing."

I laughed.

"Looking at what I'm wearing at this very moment—it's all from exes! These jeans were bought by Ollie—"

"Old fart."

"We were on ski vacation and I'd packed poorly. I was freezing and he took me into a little boutique and bought me these. They're so comfy, I could never trash them."

In fact, the Joe's brand jeans were my go-to pair. I probably wore them too much but they made my butt feel flawless.

"He was so controlling." Amber shook her head.

"My earrings? A blind date I went on."

"What kind of maniac brings a blind date a gift?"

"I know. What if…I lacked ears?!"

"They look pricey."

"I looked them up online—*$250*!"

Straight from Saks, the Jude Frances collection.

"Did you sleep with him?"

"He didn't even get a goodnight kiss! The date lasted less than an hour."

"Why maniacs think pricey gifts are the key to a woman's heart…"

"—or vagina!"

"…I will never know."

"These shoes were from Ricky."

"I always thought he was gay."

"Maybe he was. He bought them just because 'I thought you'd look cute in them.'"

"He was right. And definitely gay."

I mean, they were daniblack.

We walked up a busy Eighth Avenue and I saw the glowing red, white, and blue lights of every New Yorker's *least* favorite spot.

"Oh, hey, can we pop into that Duane Reade for a sec? I need to pick up my…BC."

"Why are you whispering, Cher?" Amber mock-whispered to me. "No one cares."

She was right. The streets around us were full of tourists, none of whom even looked at me. Not that there was anything to be ashamed of. Most men didn't realize this, but even when we weren't in a relationship (or slutting it up) us women were still typically on birth control.

I first started taking birth control at age fourteen. To keep my skin clear. The estrogen apparently neutralized the testosterone that caused pimples. Aside from that, it also lowered your risk for ovarian cancer. The less you ovulate, the less chance you have of getting cancerous cells in your ovaries. Birth control also made my periods lighter, less painful, and more scheduled. It made PMS almost non-existent. But yeah, of course, BC was great for…me not getting pregnant. I certainly couldn't afford to get pregnant right now, even if my window was getting smaller and smaller.

We entered Duane Reade and headed on the long walk toward the back of the store, passing the economy-sized bags of candy before cutting through the makeup aisle and rows of hair care products.

"What's your name, Miss?"

"Sheffield. S-H-E-F-*Field*."

I was buzzed and tired of spelling. It was annoying how the government and pharmaceutical industry controlled birth control. Why wasn't it over-the-counter? Condoms were. Would women somehow abuse over-the-counter BC? Pop Ortho Tri-Cyclen like Skittles just so they'd, like, *super* not get pregnant?!

It annoyed me to no end that once a month I had to waste time, money, and sanity going into Duane Reade to get my prescription filled. Dealing with the looks from the aging pharmacists, the immature snickers from the street kids hanging in the nearby soda aisle as they recognized the eggshell diskette packaging, the slow-as-molasses register women gabbing with each other instead of checking me out.

As my order was being filled, Amber, Erin, and I spent the time reading gossip mags and taking our blood pressure (125/81 for me, a little high, though probably affected by environment).

"Miss Sheffield…? Order's ready."

Luckily, I could now avoid additional human interaction once I got my pills since this location had just gotten some self-checkout machines. Or as I called them: "embarrassing purchase" machines. I snatched my pills and headed to an empty register where I slid up next to a man at the adjacent register who looked a little like a, uh…

"Cheryl?!"

It was Trevor self-checking out his own purchase: a 24-pack of Durex fruit-flavored (tropical) condoms.

"FOURTEEN. NINETY-FIVE."

The machine's robotic voice loudly spoke as Trevor swiped the bar code.

"Oh. My. God," whispered Erin, panicking.

"That asshole," Amber tensed up.

As Trevor glanced down at my birth control—the very same BC I used to use with him—and I glanced down at his massive pack of pineapple, coconut, and passion fruit-flavored condoms—ones he had never used with me—we both stood totally silent.

"PLEASE, PLACE THE CORRECT ITEM IN THE BAG. PLEASE, PLACE THE CORRECT ITEM IN THE BAG," the self-checkout machine kept repeating as Trevor scrambled to hide them. I didn't know what to say. So I accidentally said something completely honest.

"I'm glad to see you are having sex with someone. That samba chick still?"

Trevor was taken aback for a second before he exhaled and smiled.

"No. Uh, someone new. Met her at a conference."

"That's good. I hope she's not allergic to coconut."

He nodded toward my BC diskette.

"And you? For your skin?" he joked.

"For a guy."

That stopped him in his tracks. We both stood silent before he finally broke, pointing at my purse.

"Hey, the Kate Spade I got you."

"Yes. It's very…nice."

"I hope we never run each other again."

"I'll use CVS from now on."

Erin stood there stunned, like she'd ran into Bigfoot talking to the Loch Ness monster. Amber was psyched though. After Trevor left, she couldn't help herself.

"You sure showed him, Cher!"

"Oh my God, Cher," Erin noted, "I cannot believe that. What are the chances? And tropical-flavored condoms. What kind of little skank likes a kiwi up her hoo-hah?"

"It's no big deal."

"Running into an ex is always a big deal."

"They don't have to be shameful moments from your past."

I swiped my BC. "TWENTY NINE. NINETY-FIVE."

"Past relationships aren't regrettable failures, they're simply trials that helped us become the people we are today."

I threw my BC in the DR bag and proceeded to head toward the exit, but Erin grabbed me.

"Wait a sec, Cher. Did you tell Trevor you've found someone?"

"I told you earlier tonight."

"You *implied* you were *casually* with a guy. Not that you've met someone you're *casually* having lots of…*unprotected* sex with!"

"I never said I was."

"Oh my God! Are you going to marry this guy?!"

"Maybe."

"When can I meet him?"

"Soon."

"When?!" Amber looked leery.

"Maybe we'll catch up with him tonight…"

I reached down and looked at my phone.

"I can't wait for your wedding!" Erin was always so overzealous.

"What? Wait. Why?"

"It'll be so much fun!"

"No it won't."

"It won't?!"

"No. Not for you."

"Why?"

"No one cares about a wedding."

"That's not…"

"No one cares about a wedding except the bride."

"That's not true."

"Yes. It is."

chapter eleven

ONLY THE BRIDE CARES ABOUT HER WEDDING

…you looked gorgeous up there, Patti.

WOW. That's Vera Wang? Custom made? WOW. No wonder.

No wonder you spent so much on it. No, you're right, $10,000 is *so reasonable* for your special day.

No wonder you put us in these grey gowns. A perfect accent to yours. Oh, they're technically silver? Nice. Silver should really be the gold medal. But, of course, how could we ever show you up?

No wonder everyone in the church thought you looked like a celebrity. Everyone said that. I swear. I heard references to Katie and Cate and Kate even. A princess. I heard that. Yep, an *authentic* princess.

Whatever the case, you looked beautiful up there on the altar. Better than a celebrity or a princess. Just so…*you*.

No, I thought Jake looked fine too. Handsome. Yes, even with that skinny tie. It wasn't silly. Oh, of course, I agree with you a vest would have looked better. More formal. You're totally right, it's what separates a tuxedo from a mere suit. Really, that was a rental? I'm surprised you allowed him to. Men's Warehouse? No, I couldn't tell. I swear. But, what do I know about men's suits, you know? Yes, you're right to be a little perturbed.

Relax. I really don't think the lack of vest ruined anything. I swear, hon, I didn't hear one person talking about it. Maybe they were being polite, but I don't think there were even any whispers. I don't think it ruined anyone's enjoyment of such a beautiful ceremony. The focus was all on *you*.

I know, the focus is supposed to be all on you, and your new husband, but mainly you, so it matters what you think the most. I'd put it aside and quit thinking about it. None of us are as peeved at Jake's decision not to wear a vest as you.

He's your new husband!

You're more mad at the church, though? How do you get mad at a church? OK, yes, it was hot, you're right. But it wasn't that bad. Turn of the century churches rarely have AC, correct? Did you never investigate that when you were looking for a spot? No, I'm not blaming you. OK, I'll blame your planner. Yes, she does look like a bitch. Whatever the case, it is a gorgeous location. Though it was a tad hard to get to. Dirt road to ferry and then…no, I didn't mean that. I meant that in a good way. Romantic and isolated. Like, it made it a far more special journey for us all. But, yes, who would think it would be so hot inside the church when it's so…well…

It's a crisp fall day, look. No, I wasn't judging your date. October is a fine time for a wedding. Totally original. I don't think I've ever been to an October wedding. The fact that it's on Halloween? Even better. Really, some kids were in costumes? Totally didn't notice. I didn't even realize kids were invited. I know summer can be more expensive. I'm not calling your parents cheap, you know I love them. Plus, after the ten grand dropped on the Vera…uh, fall is nice. Much nicer than summer. Summer is trite. *Everyone* does summer.

Hannah took your original date? Shit. Bitch.

So, uh, the floral arrangements look nice. What are those? Baby's breath?

Ah…*hydrangeas.* Sorry. I'm not exactly a horticulturist.

Hydrangeas are much more expensive you say. Well, yes, I guess it is wise to buy the most exotic flowers you can. Flowers are always one of the key things I remember from any wedding. Wise to spend 25% of your budget on them. Because they'll be around a long, long time…

Just like your marriage to Jake!

The priest was so nice. A very long sermon. I felt like I learned a lot about…Catholicism. Really didn't expect to learn so much today. Yes, I guess he did kind of take away from your special day by showboating up there and pushing his own socio-political church agenda. Really, he said that? I…didn't notice. Was he your childhood priest?

Oh.

I'm sorry to hear that. Terrible. While giving a sermon? No? While teaching your pre-cana class? Really? Wow. What exactly is that, by the way? Oh, seriously? *All* Catholics have to go to an actual marriage class before they can get married? For three months?! In the year 2014?

But, wait, how would a virgin priest teach you…uh, you know, never mind.

Still, his sermon may have been long, but the vows were great. Did you write them yourself? I figured. Sounded just like *you*. Oh, really. You think he just stole them off the internet? Well, you know *men*. Jake isn't much of a creative sort, is he? I suppose you could Google some keywords and see if they check out. I hear that's what college profs are doing nowadays. Hopefully there weren't any copyright lawyers invited at least, am I right?

Oh honey, I was just kidding! That was just one of my stupid jokes! You know my stupid jokes. I make them when I'm nervous.

Don't cry.

Cry tears of joy if anything!

Yes, I deserve that.

Right, I'm sorry.

I know you had lots of other friends you could have chosen

as a bridesmaid. I really do. And I'm *totally* honored. That was so fun taking all those pictures for…two whole hours. Outside. Under the big, bright sun in the crisp fall air. They're gonna look great in your album.

I know.

I know.

You should never kid about a wedding. I wasn't thinking because…well, I'm not lucky enough to have been so blessed with this opportunity just yet in my own life.

Yes, they are indeed *highly serious* affairs.

You're right, again. When you laugh at weddings you're devaluing the whole affair, the whole institution, the whole future life of the bride and groom!

You're sullying the sanctity.

It's bad karma, yes, I agree.

…

…

Well…

…

Um…

…

My drink's empty…and I guess it's almost time for you to be introduced to the guests.

Great liquor selection here by the way. Top shelf, top notch. I think I'll go squeeze in another rosé.

OK, no, I won't I guess.

Yes, I *promise* not to get too drunk before my speech. *Nothing* will appear on YouTube.

Believe me, I have so many beautiful things to say about this beautiful event and you, my beautiful, beautiful friend. Thanks for helping me edit it. That was nice of you.

You truly are blessed.

What a great day.

For *all* of us.

📍 **Patti's** (w. 52nd St. and Broadway) | 9:38 PM

chapter twelve

GROSS CHICKS

"But it doesn't have to be that way, Cher. For *us*."

I wondered if that was true. I wondered what my wedding might eventually look like.

We were on the elevator headed up to Patti's apartment. A mom and her little boy joined us, the little boy begging his mom to let him push the fifth-floor button.

"Don't say I didn't warn you."

"We'll be quick."

"It's never quick."

"Patti used to be quick."

"Her life used to be the same as ours. Then, boom, it all changed."

"It all changed, but Cheryl…her life was *never* the same as ours."

"We should have never agreed to come over. On a Friday night?! I hope she at least has something to drink."

Patti greeted the three of us at the door and led us into her gorgeous apartment. We entered to find Christina already there, in the middle of loudly gabbing about a new guy she was seeing. And by "seeing," I meant: seeing naked. Pretty much exclusively.

They'd yet to have a date out in the real world. So they were actually about as non-exclusive as two people who only saw each other naked could be.

"It's like, I don't even know what his fashion sense is like, because I pretty much only see him in his underwear."

"Well what brand are those?" Erin idly wondered.

"Under Armour so, hmmm…"

I laughed. "He wears sporting goods as underwear…?"

"Yeah."

"Is he in shape?"

"No." She laughed. "He's kind of a fatass."

Christina took a sip from a flute of what I thought was champagne.

"I'll have a champagne too, if you don't mind, Pat."

Patti looked embarrassed.

"It's not champagne. It's Diet Sprite. Sorry. We…don't keep much alcohol in the house ever since the little bean was born."

Just then, Amber let out a huge burp.

"Well that's what I think about that!"

"Feel better, Amber?"

"The best. Though I would feel better if I'd brought some vodka. This is like hanging out with your parents when you're in high school."

If men only knew what we said, what we did, and what happened when women got together without them. They wouldn't believe it. You see, men would be surprised to learn that women, when they were away from men, just loved to be anatomically gross. It was so freeing. We loved to burp and fart. And once Amber opened the floodgates, we were all soon burping and farting up a storm inside Patti's apartment. Jake was out of town for the weekend, at a bachelor party in Montreal, and with Patti home alone with newborn Abby, she had decided it might be nice if her closest friends came over to pay her a visit. That's how it worked once you became a mother. You just decided when your friends would come to you.

Back earlier in the week, back when we had agreed to this,

via a group email of course, it had seemed like something nice to do. We hadn't seen Patti in ages, it was becoming hard to even call her a "good" friend any more, so we wanted to be good and go see her. At least I did back mid-week, when the weekend and *legitimate* fun seemed far, far away.

Of course, by now, Erin and I were a little drunk and a lot more interested in continuing our night out in the real world than visiting this artificial mommy world. But Patti sounded so desperate in her text ("when r u guys coming???") that we had to go. We had to let a stay-at-home-mom turn us into come-to-her-home friends. And, now we were being gross women inside that very home.

"He texts me such dirty stuff," Christina continued.

"Like pics of his shower curtain?"

"No! Like…Saturday afternoon he was like…'I'm horny, let's play.'"

"And…?"

"I grabbed a cab and went over to his place."

"Gross."

Patti flapped her left boob out to feed Abby, barely mumbling, "Do you mind?" We were longtime girlfriends so I'd seen her boobs many times before, just never in such a situation. I didn't even care if it was "natural." Something like that would never be natural to me, even if it was my own baby sucking my own mommy boob.

"You want to talk about gross? I found a used condom in the trash can by his bed. And it hadn't been used on me."

"Gross!!!"

"Did you still…go through with it?" Patti wondered.

Christina shrugged. She was a manhunter too. It was a sickness. This need for constant male attention.

"What can I say…? I wanted some. Plus, I'd already spent twelve bucks on cab fare."

"Gross!"

"I made him shower first! I mean, we…*did* it in the shower first."

Patti put a fully fed Abby up to her shoulder so she could burp her. Patti's apartment had begun to smell. The floor was covered with a primary color rainbow of children's toys, looking like a tornado had swept through the apartment.

"Yeah, well, I'd love to still have a little of that in my sex life," Patti wistfully noted.

Patti was the most glamorous girl I'd ever known, a total prima donna just a few years ago, and now her apartment was a complete romper room of children's toys, children's clothes, children's messes. If I didn't know better I would have thought fifteen babies lived here. A Saturday night and she was clad in a Brown University hooded sweatshirt and elastic waistbanded "jeans."

"You and Jake don't any more?" Erin wondered.

"You can't. Really. Who's gonna watch Abby, and my vagina is still…well, we haven't had sex since I was four months pregnant which…do the math: five plus seven. Twelve months! A whole year. I might as well be back in junior high. He barely touches me any more." She looked down at Abby. "But, I don't blame him. I feel so gross. I'm just a mommy now. And not even a MILF."

I'd never seen someone so sad to not be called a MILF. The room was tense, no one sure what to say. Amber farted.

"Sorry. We all had fondue for dinner…"

I was one of those girls who prided herself on being "real" around men. A cool girl. But that wasn't true. Nor was it true for 99.9% of women who said likewise. We could proclaim we were real, but real wasn't always dainty and sexy. Sure, farts were hilarious, both sexes agreed on that, but relationships weren't built on fartastic hilarity.

Cristina looked at Erin. "By the way, I hear you're single again."

"That. Is true."

"Then can I give you some advice?"

Erin looked cautiously toward me, before returning her glance to Cristina. "Yes. Please do."

Cristina ripped a loud fart and started loudly laughing. "*That's* my advice. Stay single."

We always say, "I just want to be with someone who makes me laugh." Sure, but not if he's Bozo the Clown. Not if she tries to make you chuckle with a room-clearing toot. Men were allowed to be gross. It was even sexy in a certain, *perverse* way. A gross man was saying to women of the world, "I'm so cocky I can lift my leg like a dog and let one fly and I don't even think you'll leave me." But women couldn't do that. Not even necessarily because men were truly grossed out by us being gross. Mind you, these are the same creatures that go months without laundering their jeans and seem to spend a quarter of their lives in locker rooms. No, men didn't like women being gross because they thought they weren't *supposed* to. Men thought they were supposed to be grossed-out by a woman that burped, pooped, and farted, even though they knew it had to happen behind their backs.

Sadly, modern relationships were too often based on people doing what they thought they were "supposed to" do. Erin always did, and I had finally just stopped. It occurred to me, there was just one place men liked women to be proudly "gross": the bedroom. It was how Abby had surely been born. And Cristina had long proven herself to be incredibly, grossly accomplished in that regard. It was the only way she could even get men to stick around.

God, the room was really starting to stink.

"Erin! Was that…you?!"

Erin turned bright red.

"Why…I…NO! Of course not! I wouldn't do that. I don't do that. I'm grossed out by all of you."

We laughed at Erin. She could be so childish.

"You think it's funny? You're all burping and farting, Cristina's telling disgusting hook-up stories, Patti has her boob hanging out…"

"I have to!"

"The only girl not gross here is…Abby!"

Erin pointed at the baby just as Patti realized something.

"Ooooooh. I know what that stinky smell is!"

She walked over to Abby and picked her up off her play mat.

"Abigail, did somebody poopy? I think Abigail poopied. Did you poopy Abigail? Yes, you did poopy Abigail."

She held the baby's butt to her face and sniffed, nodding toward us with an odd smile.

"Oh yeah. It was Abby."

Patti subtly passed the baby's butt near Erin's face as she took it toward the bathroom, laughing as Erin retracted in horror.

"See, Erin, we're all gross women."

"I'm not."

"If you're newly single, you should be," Amber added.

"Why?"

"Because grossness is a sign of relaxation. And if you can't be gross around your besties, how else will you build up the ability to be gross around the man of your dreams?"

"My dream is that a man never sees me gross. *Ever*. Grossness strips the romance."

"It's the reverse. You need to be gross to find perfect love, hon," called out Patti.

"I disagree!"

"Trust us!" shouted Patti from the back room.

"What does she know? She hasn't had sex in a fuckin' year," whispered Erin.

Amber smiled. "My advice to you, Erin? Start farting."

"No."

"Come on. FART."

Erin was getting redder and redder in the face, turning from Jackie to RFK to JFK and finally Teddy. I didn't agree with Amber or Patti, but I liked seeing Erin uncomfortable. So I lied.

"Come on, Erin. Amber's right. Our night needs to march on but you're not getting the marching orders until you fart. I need you to fart. Fart!"

"Yeah, Erin. Be gross for once. Fart!"

"Fart!" I began chanting.

"Fart!!" shouted Patti from the other room.

"Fart!"

"Fart!!"

"FART!!!"

We were banging our Diet Sprite-filled champagne flutes on the coffee table in chanting rhythm.

Patti peeked her head into the room, holding a balled-up diaper.

"Would you be careful with those stems. They're quite delicate."

"So am I!!!" shouted Erin.

chapter thirteen
BOOK CLUBBED

Back walking in the Hell's Kitchen night, Erin was still red in the face, traumatized by what we had made her do.

"Don't you feel better?" I smiled at her, but she didn't respond. She looked like she'd just gone through a sorority hazing. Finally she spoke up.

"This *fresh* air feels nice. Nice and clean."

We'd left Amber back at Patti's and now walked down Ninth Avenue just the two of us again. It did feel nice. We came upon a pop-up book stand and I had to stop.

"Sorry, you know I can't help myself."

I glanced at the table. *The Alchemist*, *Meditations*, Obama's biography. I grabbed a worn copy of *Siddhartha* from the table. 99 cents. Then I saw it...

Insatiable.

"Oh. My. God. Erin!"

"What?"

"Have you heard about this?"

"Chick lit."

"The best!"

"You like chick lit?"

"I like *this* lit. My friend Hannah has this book club and…"

* * *

…they meet one Sunday per month.

Sundays were perfect because that was the day their husbands watched the NFL in fall/winter and golfed at Canoe Brook Country Club in spring/summer. But, now that a few of them had babies, a few more were expecting, and all the rest were "trying," the book club had become one part baby group as well.

All the crying and noisy coddling didn't even matter, because they rarely talked books at book club. They rarely even read them. *The Goldfinch*, *Gone Girl*, *Lean In*, no one had read any of these three previous books. Except Hannah.

Hannah had been a junior lit agent at ICM who had put aside publishing industry dreams to be a stay-at-home-mom to Sofie. But she still loved to read books and still loved to talk literature. Unfortunately, none of her mommy friends really did.

These were smart, highly educated women full of excuses about having too much "on their plate" to read an entire book. Hannah lived the same life as them and wanted to snap back about how easy they actually had it: changings, feedings, putting the baby "down," then hours upon hours of free time. But Hannah knew the real reason no one in the group read any more: their brains were turning to mush.

Hanging around babies and other stay-at-homes did not keep the mind sharp. Hannah had watched her friends go from witty and bright to dull and lunkheaded. Her early assignments for the group attempted to counter this. She had assigned hard, complex books that would force her friends to flex their atrophying brain muscles. Stuff by Jonathan Franzen and David Foster Wallace, Jeffrey Eugenides and Junot Diaz and, of course, Jennifer Egan, a client at her former agency.

But, the complaints immediately rolled in: too long, too many "vocab" words, too hard to follow, what's with all the…

footnotes?! These were women who had scored in the 90th-plus percentile on the verbal portion of their SATs and now couldn't even read slightly "hard" books. So, Hannah gave up, relaxed her standards, and decided to try a more baby steps approach for these babies with babies. She started assigning easy-to-read, mainstream books she still respected (somewhat) the literary merits of. No one even read those. Or, they simply went to the movie adaptation during "date night" at the Short Hills Mall.

Thus, "book club" had become a place only to eat and gab. Most women didn't even lug their books along any more. Some, like college kids with senioritis, quit buying the books altogether. The rotating host would usually lay out a spread of bagels and muffins plus Greek yogurt and fruit for those women skipping carbs to try and lose the baby weight, and around noon champagne corks would pop for the non-breastfeeding women who could drink mimosas.

Talk would start like it always did among mothers—about being mothers. Bugaboo strollers and SnugRide car seats, Butterfly Garden baby swings and Petunia Pickle Bottom diaper bags. There was a constant swapping of hand-me-down clothing too. Even though these women were all quite rich they still maintained a certain suburban frugality.

Of course, once the bubbly started bubbling to their heads, the talk of Bugaboo strollers ceased and instead their conversations turned to sex. It always did. Suburban housewives are the horniest. Their husbands likewise with so much "on their plate"—and now-longer daily commutes to Manhattan—they rarely had time for sex any more.

Erin, Hannah told me all this as we drank wine at Corkbuzz a few Saturday nights ago.

"I've grown to believe women are too busy to read the books I assign because every time they put their babies down…they pull out Big Baby to tickle their cervix."

I laughed. Hannah had been allowed to pay a rare visit to the city for a "girls' night out" courtesy of her "hubby" Davis agreeing to babysit for the night.

"Cher, my book club friends, when they get drunk, their lips get loose. And they'll actually admit what they masturbate to. Nothing that would surprise you: movie stars, hunks in magazine ads, maybe the cute barista at the Starbucks next to the baby gym. But now..." Hannah smiled quite proudly, "they're flicking it to a *book*."

She pulled a crisp paperback from her purse and slapped it on the bar. The cover depicted luxurious bed sheets all mussed up, the imprint of two bodies still fresh in them. *Insatiable*, it was called, by H.M. Ivy.

"At first I didn't know what to think...about us reading and discussing erotica. My book club was supposed to be classy! But my friends love it, and it's the first book they've actually wanted to discuss."

"It sounds like *50 Shades*."

"*Insatiable* makes *50 Shades* seem like a junior high kid's love notes."

I didn't know what to think. I'd never read erotica. It looked cheesy and poorly written. The only women I ever saw reading it were old slobs at the airport. How humiliating to schlep around a book with such a cheesy harlequin cover. And yet, I brought a copy home.

"What's that book?" he wondered as I tipsily slid into bed later that night.

"Hannah gave it to me. It's the new hotness in the 'burbs." I embarrassingly held up the copy of *Insatiable*.

"Is that...a romance novel?"

"Apparently every horny homemaker in Short Hills is reading it."

"Then maybe we should too!"

Now we didn't read it out loud, that would have been way cheesy, we just each silently read it simultaneously. He held the book and we just read. I was slightly faster than him so when he got to each page's end, he could always feel comfortable in turning it since I was surely done by then.

The first ten pages or so, after every page, we both felt the need to make comments about how cheesy the writing was, how unbelievable the plotting was, but once we reached chapter three and the first sex scene between housewife Veronica and barista Marco we were hooked. And so turned on.

We had some wild sex that night and then, in our post-coital snuggles, immediately jumped back into reading the book and working ourselves up all over again.

I never realized how much I liked graphic tales of sex. Maybe all women did. Was that why we never minded when guys would try to be gross and tell sex stories from their pasts? Even though it shouldn't have turned us on, and should have totally turned us *off*, was it having the opposite effect? Personally, I didn't minded hearing tales from *his* past. They excited me. They excited me that he was such a coveted man. That he was such a coveted man that now coveted me and only me.

Before we went to sleep that night, as I lay *Insatiable* on the nightstand, staring at its cover for one more second before I clicked off my lamp, I noticed the author's name and a light bulb went off:

H.M. Ivy.

📍 **Rudy's** (w. 44th St. and Ninth Ave.) | 11:21 PM

chapter fourteen
SITCOM SITUATIONS

"Do you understand? H.M. Ivy."

"The author? What?"

"Hannah Marie Hefner."

"OK…"

"From the *Ivy* League."

"No!"

I smiled, surprised Hannah had kept it from me for so long.

"Hannah finally figured out how to get her book club to read a book. *Her* book!"

We now stood on Ninth Avenue next to a five-foot-tall statue of a pantsless cartoon pig named Rudy. The pig wore a red tuxedo jacket with a bow tie, his right hand slightly upturned in a pageant contestant wave. Rudy's bar was an iconic mainstay in the neighborhood, but that didn't mean most people ever ventured inside.

"We should go in here."

The pig had a small smirk on his face; Erin did not as we entered and were immediately slapped in the face with the smell.

"You make me feel all…*under*-sexed with that book club story and then bring me to this dump? It smells like a men's locker room."

"How would you know?"

Erin looked around leerily, until something caught her eye. "Oh my God, it's those guys from Drunx!"

I was about to approach them when Erin put her hand on my upper arm, stopping me.

"Don't! They probably think we're total stalkers!"

"Did they even see us at Drunx? Guys don't notice anything."

"You don't know that!"

"Who cares?"

"What if they think we're following them?"

"They'll be excited. Let's get some drinks and talk to them."

"What should I say?"

"The first thing that comes to your mind."

As we sidled up beside the two men, I couldn't help but notice how pathetic the one guy looked—the guy I had called a "tool" earlier—all hunched over his bar stool with a raggedy, corrugated cardboard box full of junk on the bar top in front of him. Then, Erin blurted out the first thing that must have come to her mind:

"You just get laid off?"

The tool looked surprised, before turning to his friend as if to say, "What do I do *now*?" He looked back toward us, only able to muster a pathetic "Huh?"

His handsome friend turned with a mischievous grin on his face, before grabbing his iPhone, illuminating the screen, and then shining it toward our faces as if it was a spotlight and we were movie stars. I rolled my eyes at him and Erin quickly pushed the phone spotlight away.

"I said, uh, 'Did you just get laid off…'"

Erin began brazenly rifling through the poor guy's cardboard box. She became another person when she was trying to flirt with guys.

"…from the best job in the world?!"

In the box were typical items of dude-ness. A plastic basketball hoop, some old tees and boxers, CDs and DVDs, a box of condoms, and a bottle of what looked like expensive bourbon.

"Uh…"

The man didn't know what to say, clearly intimidated by Erin if not *all* women. He wasn't even sure if he was being mocked or not. I wasn't quite sure either. I cut in:

"So what's your stories?"

They introduced themselves as Les and Devin. Les explained that he hadn't been laid off. He had just been dumped by his girlfriend. Thus, that box was a dump box. That immediately gave Erin a connection to him.

They continued talking while I danced between catching the bartender's eyes and Devin's.

"A PBR and a Moscow Mule," I quickly ordered when the bartender finally turned my way.

As I studied Devin's eyes, my own eyes diverted and I couldn't help but notice that Erin and Les were actually seeming to hit it off. The recently relationshipless. Erin, possibly drunker than I thought, began to now pull individual items out of the box like she was at a rummage sale, Les offering a brief footnote to what each was and what it represented.

"You're quiet."

I turned to Devin, him finally having acknowledged me.

"Just thinking."

"About what?"

I smiled at him.

"About the first step of a relationship becoming more serious, but not yet *fully* serious…"

"What's that?"

I nodded toward Les and his box.

"Moving random stuff into each other's places."

Devin mulled it over. "Like what?"

"Well first, it starts simple. You get sick of waking up in the morning and being forced to finger brush your teeth—or use *his* gnarly brush."

Devin laughed. "Gnarly, huh?"

"You get bored with not having some of your own entertainment materials lying around for when your partner's sleeping and you're still awake."

"You get tired of having to put your jeans back on to venture out of the bedroom to the bathroom, lest *her* nosy roommate runs into you in your birthday suit when it's not even your birthday!"

I nodded. "Exactly! So you buy a second toothbrush to leave in her bathroom. A pair of jammy shorts and a comfy tank top for lounging around his place."

"You secretly shove it into the corner of one of his drawers without even asking until he formally gives you a full drawer with his full blessing."

I laughed.

"Let me apologize for all women." I shook my head. "What a total sitcom situation."

"Sitcom situation?"

"Yeah, like on TV. Most steps of love are, I'm just now beginning to realize."

Nowadays, we didn't live real situations and then watch sitcoms comment on them. Instead, sitcoms created phony situations and then we all tried to stupidly live up to them. Or *down* to them. A sitcom devotes a whole half-hour to the so-called stresses of moving some stuff into your new boyfriend's place, and then we are all dumb enough to think that was something we should stress out about too.

You had to remember, the goal of sitcoms is completely opposite from the goals of real life. The goal of real life is carpe diem. To seize the day. The goal of sitcoms is the reverse. Not to tell a succinct story, but rather to stretch that story out as long as humanly possible.

So there is no love at first sight. Two beautiful characters meet each other at the grocery store or on the studio set's indoor sidewalk or, most likely, at the place they both work and which created the punny title of the program, and though thunderstruck with what most human beings would recognize as feelings of romantic attraction, or at least stirrings of sexual desire, they neglect those sensations. That wouldn't work on a sitcom. The episode would be over before the opening credits. There would be no reason for a season, ad money, and an attempt to reach 100 episodes and syndication so the sitcom could start running ad nauseum on TBS and TNT. Thus, sitcom characters had to reject their natural, mutual, and romantically scripted feelings and let them manifest another way. This was known as: Sexual Tension.

Something that has *only* ever existed on sitcoms, and maybe middle school rollerskating parties.

Mike & Maddy, Ross & Rachel, everyone on the cast of *How I Met Your Mother*. Instead of just dating, or just sleeping together and getting it over with, these perfect-for-each-other(-and-the-audience) matches have to have an excuse *not* to get together. That excuse, was, and usually is: Hate.

An artificial hate that usually lasts an entire season of "will they or won't they?" finally reaching a fever pitch with a fight. An unexpected kiss. A return the next season ("Three months later") as a couple. The entire show now a whole lot more boring with a whole new set of sitcom situations:

*When (and who will be the first) to say "I love you"

*When to tell their friends (also known as the only other characters on the show)

*When to move in together and to whose absurdly-large-for-this-city apartment

Season 3 arguments. Season 4 mini-breakup. Season 5 now best friends as they watch each other date and flounder with other people (usually A-list guest stars). Season 6 back together. Season 7 wedding. Season 8 a baby. Season 9 everyone now hates these once-beloved characters. Season 10 no one is watching any more and is stunned to learn the show is still on the air.

I loved sitcoms, but they had never taught me how to love

correctly. Maybe unsurprisingly, I wasn't sure they had taught anyone anything. I knew I could do better. I was a child of the '80s who loved laugh track crap like *Growing Pains*, *Who's the Boss?*, and of course *The Facts of Life*. But I knew my real life could be funnier, my love life more realistic.

"Getting dumped, I might as well be dead. What should I do…?" I overheard Les complain to Erin and my thoughts were interrupted.

Les was a classic sitcom character and I was starting to love him all the more for that. Nerds were often sitcom-y in their romantic and sexual interactions, frequently whining like his words were coming out of, not his own mouth, but a writer's room in Santa Monica.

Erin held in her hands a *The Godfather* box set she'd just removed from Les's dump box.

I eyed Devin and smiled at him as I grabbed my beer and Erin's drink, handing it back to her before looking Les in the eye. With my free right hand I grabbed Les by his collar and shook him hard, as I quoted that famous line from *The Godfather*, one of my favorite movies.

"You can act like a man!!! What's the matter with you? Is this how you turned out? A Hollywood *finocchio* that cries like a woman?"

Devin immediately burst out laughing. Erin looked at me like, "What the hell are you doing?"

I didn't quite know what the hell I was doing. It just seemed right. Erin tried to recoup.

"She's right. You have to burn that box of stuff, Les." Erin grabbed a book of matches off the bar top and wiggled them in front of his face. He looked unsure.

"That's what I've been saying all night, bud!" Devin exclaimed.

"Come on, Les. Let's go outside now and handle it."

"I…don't…"

The funny thing was, I would soon be a Hollywood *finocchio* myself.

My sitcom pilot (working title: *The Man of My Dreams*) had just been acquired by Lionsgate that very morning. The pilot was slated to start shooting in September. At age thirty-two I had finally "made it." I was almost certainly going to have to move to Los Angeles. I didn't want to. I loved New York. And I had such an important reason not to ever want to leave here.

"I don't know, guys. I'm just not sure I was actually even *dumped*."

I turned toward Les, and said:

chapter fifteen
HOW TO KNOW WHEN A WOMAN IS ABOUT TO DUMP YOU

YOU WERE DUMPED.

Les, women do all the breaking up and you'll fully know when it was done to you.

In fact, some statistical studies put us chicks as the ones ending 80-90% of heterosexual relationships. We'll get to "Why?" in a second. But, Les, at least if you are about to become one of those 80-90% dumped, or already *were*, you should be able to see the warning signs.

DECISION-MAKING
Remember, women take forever to make a decision. Watch your girlfriend hem and haw over which toaster to buy or which flavor of ice cream to grab, and then ask yourself: how long would it take this same creature to go from thinking she should end things with you to actually ending them? *Months*. Men, on the other hand, make snap decisions out of pure, heated emotion. Or, usually, they make no decision at all. They just let things slowly fizzle out, which is why they rarely do the breaking up.

LACK OF SEX

This is obvious, but if she's thinking about dumping you then she's growing disgusted by you and will be repulsed by even your most mild touch. Sex becomes a chore at best. Does she flinch when you try to rub her neck? Pull away quickly when you hug her? Turn her cheek when you try to kiss it? Does she ever say something as blunt as: "Not now, I'm going to sleep. Feel free to jerk off, though"? Then again, don't confuse her having tons of sex with you as still loving you. She might just be covering her tracks and getting you off the scent. Women can be devious.

SLOW COMMUNICATION

Now, Reagan was known as The Great Communicator, but women are the Frequent Communicators. The only creatures on earth who can turn a "How are you?" into a two-hour phone call where you don't speak even once. We love to talk. We love to quickly answer texts, reply to emails, IMs. We don't play games like men. We don't wait a certain amount of time. Or not respond in order to seem hard to get. If we have something to say, we say it. So when your girlfriend, who used to respond to all your communications within minutes, starts taking hours, just know: the end is near.

THE STAND UP

This will let you know you have a week left *at best*. You and your *amore* make plans to dine. And then, once you're there, sitting at the bar having a beer while you wait for her, you get a text: "running late." No prob. Another beer. Half-hour later: "coming soon." Sure. That's cool. Several more delaying texts, and two to three hours later, she arrives. She decided she was having too much fun at The Smith to keep her date with you at The Stag's Head. When she still loved you, she would have. If she still loved you, she certainly would have. But now that she's about to dump you, she has no interest in making you happy.

LISTEN TO WHAT SHE SAYS

Of course, the easiest thing to do is to quit dicking around with your iPhone, mindlessly watching the game over her shoulder, and start listening to her. Listen to her thoughts, her worries, her fears. Notice when she cries and what makes her angry. She's not flat-out telling you—but she's *telling* you, Les. Remember, she doesn't want to break up with you! And she's trying her best to tell you what to do so that doesn't happen. Listen to her, dammit! Listen to her from now on!

    Ah…but I know you won't, Les.
    "I promise I will. From now on."
    "No you won't. Then, you'll get dumped again and act surprised again. You'll call her a crazy bitch to Devin. Then, you'll start the cycle over again with some other poor chick."
    I was worried it might be Erin.
    "No! I swear I won't. This is good advice."
    "OK, I believe you. But, remember, don't say I didn't warn you."

📍 **Rudy's** (w. 44th St. and Ninth Ave.) | 11:38 PM

chapter sixteen

SOCIAL QUEUES

After giving Les that harsh truth, I think he was scared of me. He retreated to what would surely be a more pleasant conversation with a now-apologetic Erin, while I continued my little flirtations with Devin. All the while we both snooped on our friend's conversation, seeing if they were hitting it off in any way.

"So what was Jenn like?" Erin wondered. "What kinds of girls do you typically date?"

"Devin," I whispered to him. "Here's what Les is thinking she's asking: 'Name *any* type of woman who isn't me because I will be totally creeped if you name someone who is just like me.'"

Of course, because I knew her so well I could tell Erin actually did want Les to describe someone exactly like her. She always misread what guys meant, and she never talked in a way so guys would easily know what she meant. Les seemed equally bad if not worse at such things.

I could tell, in Les's unsure, cracking voice that perhaps he wanted to describe someone exactly like her too, but that he was simply too cowardly to do that. Instead, he said something non-committal:

"Oh you know, I like girls—I mean, *women*—with a unique personality who like to have fun."

"That could describe anyone!" I shoved Devin. "Who doesn't have a unique personality?! Even if your personality is boring, it's still uniquely your own. And is there really anyone out there who prefers *not* having fun?"

Devin shrugged.

"Of course not. So what Les is essentially saying is: 'I like *all* women.'"

Devin smiled.

"And that truly means: 'I think I could like *you* if given the opportunity.'"

Now, given *this* opportunity, Erin—if she was better at reading situations—would have taken control of the conversation by implying that she could very well like him as well, e.g., "Well, I have a personality and I do like unique fun—that good enough?!"

But, instead, for just a split second, I noticed the micro-expression on her face: utter sadness. As if Les had said he hated her.

"Devin, Erin needs a guy she might be interested in to say something incredibly on-the-nose like: "I prefer tall women with sandy blonde hair who look like they do yoga and who are drinking vodka in this bar and currently talking to me this very second."

"Oh really?" Devin raised his eyebrows.

"You see, Erin listens too much to what guys say as opposed to what they do."

"That's what I always tell Les. The mere fact he's talking to her and looking her in the eye—when not nervously looking down—should tell her all she needs to know: he likes her."

"Exactly! And the mere fact Erin is fishing for Les's 'type' should likewise tell him all he needs to know: she's interested in him." I though to myself that it also clearly told me what I really wanted to know: she was at least somewhat over Joe. Good."

Instead of all that, though, Erin tried to push Les away, pointing at a really pretty blonde standing in line near the bathroom and asking of him: "Well...what about *her*?"

She was essentially saying: "What about that absolutely stunning woman over there? With her *Playboy* bunny hair, tight body, and award-winning T&A that makes me feel like an ugly duckling? Is *she* your type?"

Les's look told you all you needed to know: "*Of course* she's my type. She fits every cultural standard of beauty in the history of the world and is a billion-out-of-10 gorgeous on any scale any human culture would ever possibly use!"

But, of course, Les was too nice to say that. He was also too honest to flat-out say: "No." But not honest enough to say: "Yeah, she's super hot but I don't have a prayer with her so who cares?"

Instead, he said: "She pretty...*pretty*. If that's your thing."

"Devin, blondes with perfectly symmetrical faces and ballooning D-cups are, like, *everybody's* thing."

Devin looked me up and down. I was anything but the aforementioned, but he didn't seem to mind.

Of course, Erin misread Les's casual statement as cocky aloofness. Which was sexy to her. The fact he was so blasé and dismissive should have told her all she needed to know—that even though all of us knew the blonde was pretty, Les didn't care, he was far more interested in talking to *her*, Erin. Instead, Erin took Les's statement like he was effusively praising the blonde, and immediately went on the defensive, launching an attack with an incredibly petty line:

"Yeah, well, I would never get fake boobs myself."

Les should have taken the mere fact she was talking about boobs as a signal that, if he played his cards right he might soon be seeing her (proudly) non-fake boobs, but, instead, he got abruptly apologetic.

"I'm sorry."

"That I would never get fake boobs?!"

"No. I'm sorry for...jeez, I don't know..."

That was just forty-eight seconds of their one-on-one conversation before they both turned toward Devin and I and Erin asked:

"So…Cheryl…should we get another one…or…should we…go to another bar?"

Erin had apparently been intrigued enough by her forty-eight-second one-on-one conversation that she had begun… talking like a robot to me. As Devin and Les began chatting, she pulled me aside and quickly whispered to me.

"Should we ask them if they want to come with us to the next spot?"

"Do you want them to?"

"Well…do you think he likes me?"

Erin still had a junior high schooler's mentality about guys "liking" her and always made me do her bidding.

"Should I pass him a note in class?"

I turned to Devin and Les and spoke up.

"Erin is wondering if you creeps would like to follow us to another bar?"

Erin look mortified. So did Les. But Devin quickly threw back his drink.

"Of course we would! Right, Les? Where are we following you to?"

He crooked his eyebrows toward me.

"Actually, I have the perfect spot."

📍 **Bloopers** (w. 43rd St. and Eleventh Ave.) | 12:00 AM

chapter seventeen
THE ONLY PICK-UP LINE THAT MATTERS

Bloopers

Bar | Midtown | $$$$

Time Out rating: ★★★☆☆

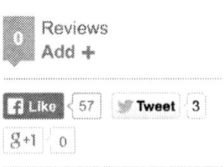

573 Eleventh Ave.
New York, NY 10036
SEE MAP
212-BLO-OPER
SEND TO PHONE

One of those "only in New York" bars, it sounded like a bit of an urban legend until crowds started gathering to see for themselves. Oh, and the crowds now pack this subversive sports bar where, during day-time hours a non-stop stream of sports (wait for it...) bloopers run looped on the joint's fifteen HD televisions. The main attraction starts at midnight, though, when the TVs are switched over to...well, you'll just have to see for yourself. That's when the XXXcellent night truly begins to take shape. Buy a pitcher of "Blooper Blonde" and check your prudeness at the door.
— Peter Landau

0 Reviews
Add +

Like 57   Tweet 3
g+1 0

Bloopers was already packed. Everyone must have read the same *Time Out New York* piece I had. All New Yorkers read the same things, yet we all thought we had brilliant "tips" no one else knew about. If bars and restaurants were truly hip, the majority of us wouldn't have even heard of them yet because the majority of us weren't hip. I certainly wasn't. If I knew of a "hip" bar by now, it had surely become or was approaching un-hip.

Up at the bar, Les and Devin tried getting us a pitcher of beer when a Big Ben-esque chime rung out. High midnight.

Everyone around the place began to titter, cutting conversations short, ignoring the need for drinks, turning their backs on the people they were currently hitting on, and instead angled their eyes upward at the numerous television screens.

Then, grainy porn footage began playing, showing a man having sex in the shower with his…well, *scene partner*. I refuse to call her a star. Erin glanced at me, her face red and mouth agape. I guess she hadn't read that same TONY article as the rest of us.

"What is *this*, Cheryl?!"

Just then, the female actress slipped on the tub's porcelain causing her to pull down the shower curtain and rod (not to mention her scene partner and his giant rod) with her all into a heaping pile. Everyone at the bar erupted in laughter, though no one louder than Erin.

Now it was my turn to stare at her with my mouth agape.

We watched a few more porn bloopers—it was impossible to look away—with Erin laughing more and more rambunctiously at each new one. Two men amongst the many noticed us laughing and approached, leaning toward me.

"Huh?"

I hadn't heard him and he used that as an excuse to lean in close, putting his left hand delicately on the small of my back, his right arm gently grasping my left bicep. A classic guy move. You couldn't hear me the first time so I guess I'll need to lean in and touch you so you can hear me this second time. Wrong!

"I *said*: 'Have you seen this one before?'" he said cockily, now adding a slight Mr. Miyagi "wax-on" massage motion to the small of my back, right where the tramp stamp would have been if I had combined miserable foresight with my teenage butterfly obsession.

I weaseled out of his grasps.

"It's, you know, a *blooper*," said Erin, cutting in, clearly repulsed by these two sleazeballs in their tight shirts.

"Oh? We thought you just looked like the kind of girls with some familiarity with these…*movies*," noted the other of man as he rattled some ice cubes around his mouth.

"Yeah right!" Erin seemed somewhat amused by the guy. The asshole. Even though he spoke in the unemotional monotone of a cult leader. I was already bored with him. I look away to see if I could find what Devin was up to.

I turned back to find Erin arguing with him about the fact that she'd told him her name, but he refused to tell her his. Some stupid game.

"OK, then if I don't get to know your name, what should I call you?" Erin asked.

"You can call me 'Don't-Know-My-Name.' And you can call my friend 'Don't-Know-His-Name.'"

The asshole's wingman grabbed Erin's hands and was leaning in to kiss them, when he quickly pulled away.

"I just realized I don't know where these filthy things have been!"

He wiped his own hand off on his jeans.

"Hey! They're clean." She laughed, but I was getting tired of this.

"What are your *real* names?" I sharply asked.

"Wouldn't you like to know?" cracked the asshole.

"Not really."

"Take a guess!" said his wingman.

"Why would I care to?" I wondered.

"Because if you get it right, I will grant you three wishes…"

I was bored with these guys and their lines.

Erin guessed "Charlie."

Men who used pick-up lines just didn't get it.

Erin guessed "Steve."

There are *no* pick-up lines. And there are no pick-up artists.

Especially these dilettantes. Especially these two young dorks. Still probably living in Hoboken or Queens or still in the 'burbs with mom and dad. Still probably choosing bars based purely on drink deals ($10 pitchers of Blooper Blonde) and quantity—not *quality*—of easy women.

Erin guessed "Josh" and she was wrong again.

"You lose." He smiled.

"OK, so what is it?"

"Gimme your number and I'll tell you…"

He held out a cocktail napkin and a pen. Erin smiled, thinking about it for a second, before taking the pen and jotting her number down. She looked back up at the asshole.

"So…?"

"It's Steve. You were actually right."

He laughed, snatched the napkin out of her hand, and he and his buddy headed toward the bar.

Erin looked at me.

"That was probably a mistake, huh?"

I shrugged.

"I doubt he'll ever use it."

"Really?"

"Assholes like that just get numbers to feed their egos. It makes them feel better about their pathetic lives."

"Oh…"

"It's like a one-night stand."

"When was the last time you had one of those?"

"Let's just say: it's been awhile."

chapter eighteen

THE NIGHT OF MANY STANDS

Men believe—and us women have allowed men to continue to believe—that if we sleep with you the first time we meet you, then we have no interest in a relationship with you.

Not true.

Sometimes, out of shame, we will try to turn a one-night stand into a standing relationship. But, not always. Sometimes, a stand is just a stand. I've had some memorable ones.

One-night #1: Patrick *Italian-Last-Name* was my lab partner in a blow-off earth sciences class we needed to graduate. He was cool and probably thought likewise of me. But, we never flirted on those Tuesdays and Thursdays we sat next to each other. The night before graduation, at a "Senior Saturdays" event at Philmore's Pub, with everyone laughing and crying about graduation, I stumbled into Pat. I'd never seen him outside the classroom. He looked hot. He immediately gave me a more-than-friendly hug. He was moving to Boston for a job the next week, me to New York for whatever. He poured me a plastic pint of Natty Light from his pitcher. It was warm and foamy. Closing time approached and people started pairing off for one last hurrah.

I figured why not. Why not finally see what a one-night stand was actually like? I'd been a prude for far too long. I'm still not sure if it counts as a one-night stand if you've known the person for a while, but I'd never had one before so I didn't quibble. Before I entered the real world, I wanted to find out what it was like. It was like…hot and sloppy and Pat struggling to function. In the morning I dressed quickly and slipped out of his bedroom to find his two roommates (and their extended families) in the living room preparing to go to the graduation ceremony. "Congratulations!" they all boisterously shouted. I'd look up Pat on Facebook to see how he's doing now, if I could just remember his last name. I think it ended in an "i."

One-nights #4–15: In my early New York years I had my "slut phase." We all have them. Usually when we're young, confused, and looking for love. Or validation. That's how we think it works. But I'll back up. My first six months in New York, post-college, were my scared phase. I was so overwhelmed! Living with Emily and Erin in a converted two-bedroom in Murray Hill, just trying to keep afloat as a low-paid lackey at a newspaper, so excited to go out at night. So confused too. What to wear, where to go, how to get there, what to drink, who to talk to. How to talk to men. It was so scary. In college, you just showed up at a bar, or house party, and instantly were running into friends left and right. Sure, you were occasionally nervous to talk to a cute guy you had a crush on—but it still *happened*. Not in the real world. In the real world, I had no idea how to turn these strange men into conversation partners into friends into dates into lovers into boyfriends. So, I started drinking more and more vodka tonics each night and standing in more and more prominent places in the bar and wearing less and less clothing and then just waiting for one man to talk to me. It always happened. And then…"it" usually happened. I was pathetic. Had no dignity. No discretion. But, it was thrilling! It was intoxicating. (And I was usually intoxicated.) In a way, it wasn't like I was sleeping with random men. It was like I was sleeping with New York City! A great excuse for youthful sluttiness, huh?

One-night #18: I met Ricky at my first decent-paying office job in the city, writing low-level account copy for Weber Shadwick. Ricky was in a different department but I was always so excited to run into him in the elevator for those quick seconds-long conversations. Even in these brief interactions, Ricky could always make me laugh. Then again, I was so enamored by him I would have probably pretended to keel over if he'd told me a knock-knock joke. At that year's Christmas party, we apparently made a scene drunkenly making out on the dance floor. At least that's what everyone told Ricky back at work Monday morning. I was now in my late-20s and had already decided to leave the cubicle world for good to start bartending at night so I'd have time to write during the day. So, that Christmas party was my last official work function and, thus, I guess I didn't really care about the inkwell or where I ate. Ricky must have, though, as he sent an email to the whole company Monday afternoon, apologetically but obliquely referencing the pen-dipping and the shitting ("To my colleagues, I deeply regret my disruptive behavior at this year's wonderful holiday party at the Marriot Marquis…"). Ricky pretty much forced me to pretend to be his girlfriend for the next year to save face and keep him on the fast track to becoming the eventual CFO of the company. It was a weird year of saving face after a great night of sucking face.

Honorable mention:

- That skinny French guy in Paris (#2) during a post-graduation trip.
- A regrettable blow job or two (#3, #23).
- Those blind dates where I thought we had a spark but ultimately just got played (#16, #20, #21).
- A wedding hookup or two (#17 and #19).

- That hairy (and uncircumcised) Greek guy in Athens (#22) during a girls' vacation.
- A negligible bar smooch or five (those don't deserve official numbers for my overall "number" since things like that just happen in New York).

One-night stands, a zillion standing excuses for why they happened. But, none of them very valid. Even us women know that. I'm not sure any of these stands shaped me or made me the person I am. But to quote Elton John: "I'm still standing." Though, no longer having one-night stands.

"Oh my god, I can't believe I just quoted Elton John."
"Do you regret it?"
"Quoting Elton?"
"No. '*Them*.'"
"I don't regret *them* but it's not like I'm proud."
"OK."
"I don't wish *them* to be permanently deleted from my record, but I'm sure glad they're not on the public record. They just…*are*."
"I can't believe you've had that many, Cher!"
"You haven't?! Count 'em up."
"I'd be too scared to know the truth."
"You won't give me your number?"

Just then, Devin blew past us, abruptly dragging Les out of Bloopers.

"Are you guys leaving?!" I called out as Devin flashed a smile before pushing Les through the front door.

"Are they really leaving?" Erin looked at me, confused, before sprinting out the door after them.

chapter nineteen
HOS BEFORE BROS

Moments later, Erin returned from outside, smiling.
"What happened?"
"Les lost his phone."
"Then why are you smiling?"
"Because…he then found my number."
"You'll tell him, but not me?"
"No, I meant I *gave* him my phone number."
"And…?"
"He said he'll text in a bit."
"It's already past midnight."
"That's bad?"
"Not necessarily."
"I'm realizing it might be a late night."
"It might be a *never* night."
"Why do you say that?"
"Because I think he's picking his bro before a ho."

Erin looked a little confused. I was confused about what Erin saw in Les.

"What do you mean by that? Calling me a 'ho.'"
"It's a dumb thing boys say: 'Bros before hos.' Always be loyal to your male friends over any girls. 'Hos,' in this instance,

used more out of a need for a catchy rhyme than any specific commentary on women's sexual behavior.

Once Devin and Les had left Bloopers, it had become douche central, and we really had no choice but to venture outside to look for a new spot on Tenth Avenue.

"Well I think it's stupid."

"Right? Why would you choose your stupid beer-drinking buddies over some great girl you could fuck, marry…?"

"Kill?"

"I think that saying must have been created by some loser man who couldn't get any women…"

"Most ideals are created by loser men."

"To keep their cooler friends who can actually get girls from deserting them. The same thing is true of the term 'pussy-whipped.'"

"I hate that term too. Gross."

"I know. It's like, 'Oh you're going out with a cute girl tonight as opposed to sitting around playing dumb video games with your friends? Lame. Bros before hos, dude.'"

Erin joined in.

"'What? You'd rather have dinner with the woman you love than go to two-for-one pitcher night with your buddies? Pussy-whipped, bro.'"

I laughed.

"You know what, though? I hate to admit it, but guys are kinda right. Bros should be before hos."

"Really?"

"Yes, they should. And, conversely for us, the same thing should hold true."

"'Chicks before dicks'?"

"Exactly. But it doesn't work. We'll sell a friend out in a second for some dick. Just like you sold me out to go chase down a boy you don't even really like."

"Hey! I *might* like him."

We walked silently for a bit. I thought about how so many girls I knew didn't even have friends. They just had other women they hung out with and bitched about guys with. We could be so fickle. Men (and dogs) were often considered paragons of loyalty, at least towards men, but you'll never hear such a thing said about us women. "You should meet my friend Tara—she's so…loyal." Nope. Never.

Every time a girlfriend stood me up for something we were supposed to do and I eventually found out where she actually was, a man was almost certainly involved in the equation. Which, oddly enough, made me blame the man. But I shouldn't have. Men didn't care. Hang out with me, or don't, I don't really care. But women would cancel a trip around the world just for some minor male attention.

"I'm sorry, Cher."

"It's all right. You just did what's natural."

We walked a bit longer in silence.

"What do you think…Joe is doing tonight?"

I had to laugh at the irony. I wondered if Erin was listening to anything I'd said all night. I stared at her and she became a little girl.

"Come on. Appease me."

"It's almost impossible to say."

"I know. He doesn't have much of an online presence."

"So?"

"Makes him…hard to stalk."

"Don't."

"Why?"

"Your head is in a very screwy place. Anything you're possibly imagining him doing is so much crazier than anything he's actually up to."

"Really?"

"He probably bought a six-pack at the bodega and is playing video games at some friend's apartment. Broing it up. If he was online you'd realize that."

I'm at Murph's Pad in New York, NY
swarmapp.com/laxbro5/checkin…

"He's never really been into video games."

"OK, then he bought a handle of cheap rum and is watching dumb shows on Hulu all night."

> **I'm at my cheap fouton in New York, NY (with no others) I'm watching "It's Always Sunny in Philadelphia" on @tvtag**

"He's a bourbon drinker."

Erin was starting to get on my nerves.

"Then he's been…at a shitty sports bar with 'the boys' root root rooting on the home team. The Knicks did play tonight."

> **I'm at Ship of Fools in New York, NY (with @balddork, @fratadult, and others)**

"And…?

I was flustered.

"And he'll drink pitchers of beer and shove buffalo wings in his face."

> **I just earned the Buffalo Wing Sauce on Face/No Girls in the Place badge**

"And…?"

Erin was pathetically "And? And? And?"-ing me like a child asking about the mysteries of Santa Claus.

"And what about women? Is he hitting on one already? So soon?"

"I don't know."

"Will they hit on him?"

"Not when his fingers and lips are covered in nuclear-red chicken wing sauce."

"You really think that's what he's doing? You really think that's how his night's going to end? You really think—?"

At that moment, thinking about it, I was surprised there

wasn't a social media service you could buy after a breakup that would blast out daily tweets about how you were doing something awesome, that would add false check-ins placing you at someplace awesome, and even generate Facebook pictures showing you looking awesome with someone awesome. Meanwhile, you could be sitting at home crying yourself to sleep.

"Do you think he's even out right now???"

I'd had enough. Erin needed a strong does of reality.

"I'll tell you what Joe's doing…this is a month since you broke up so he's not over you, but he's *over* you. And to a certain extent he's thrilled. He'd forgotten how to have fun. He'd forgotten the kind of life a man can live in this city. He'd just accepted being in a betrothed cage full of Seamless Web orders and reality TV shows about people trying to lose weight or make the most delicious cupcakes. And now's he relishing being back on the scene. He's making a scene. He's going out every single night. Drinking 'til close. His single friends who used to see him once a quarter now see him twice a week. He's Mr. 'Just One More.' 'Stay out, just one more. Just one more.' Until he gets so drunk he passes out. Or…gets laid."

Erin looked like she'd seen a ghost.

"You shouldn't be surprised. He may have forgotten his game while he was with you, but he's returned to a dating scene with superior assets. He's older, richer, sexier, more mature, more empathetic, better at talking to women. You may have been through with him, but don't be confused, he's a serious catch. The older they are, the catchier they get. Especially to younger women. Women with taut skin, meager bank accounts, bendy limbs, good aerobic stamina, and voracious sexual appetites. These are the women who now pursue him—and vice versa. The good news is: he doesn't want a relationship. Just *a lot* of fun."

"How is that a good thing?!"

She looked really upset.

"Because he's just begun his Year of Being Ridiculous."

chapter twenty
THE YEAR OF BEING RIDICULOUS

She told him she used to go on school ski trips simply for the sexual exploration.

"It was certainly better than any sex-ed class."

Several times a winter, her Pike Middle School's ski club would take a bus trip to Stowe, Vermont, a few hours north. The morning leg was uneventful, young kids still bleary-eyed as the bus left before sunrise. But the late evening return trip, also in the dark, was what everyone would eagerly await. It was the reason boys and girls who didn't like to ski, or even know how, went.

Boys and girls would pair off, two to a seat, and engage in making out, heavy petting, and hand jobs. Never oral sex. Never *sex* sex. ("I was only thirteen!" she shouted when he questioned her on that point.) But lots and lots of hand jobs.

"So…you'd just have your hand wrapped around a tiny dick? Out in the *open*?!" he crassly asked. Then again, she had been the one being crass.

"Yes. But everyone was doing it."

"Where did they…?!"

"Into a sock."

"Wait. You're telling me, just as he was about to come, he'd reach down, rip of his shoes and sweaty ski socks, and aim into that?!"

She lifted her head off his chest and looked him in the eye like he was an absolute idiot.

"Of course not. *Another* sock. A fresh sock from his bag."

"I probably have socks older than you."

He always said that corny line. They'd first met on his 32nd birthday. She was just twenty-three, a few months into living her New York City life.

She was younger than he was but no dope. She'd gone to a better university than he had, at least according to *U.S. News & World Report*. But, though she'd been putting her hand on penises since bat mitzvah age, she was relatively inexperienced. She'd only lost her virginity four-and-a-half years earlier, during the second semester of her freshman year of college and to her second semester boyfriend. The ensuing four years of sexual experience were also with college kids—overeducated nerds—who were terrible in the twin sack.

But now she was having amazing sex with an older man. "You have an amazing *cock*," she'd say, even realizing how ridiculous that sounded as it came out of her mouth. But that whole year was ridiculous.

This was his Year of Being Ridiculous, he often told her, which should have hurt her feelings, but didn't. He'd just split with his fiancée, a woman his own age he had been with for four years, and now he was back on the prowl.

On his 31st birthday he'd had a $300 prix fixe at Daniel with his then-girlfriend. (A dinner that, at that time in her life, cost half her rent, she'd calculated when he told her the story.) On his 31st birthday he thought he was dining with the only women he'd ever live with, sleep with, and have sex with for the next sixty birthdays. But, by his 32nd birthday, he was single and drinking at The Ginger Man with a wild bunch of equally single male friends.

He hadn't planned to meet any girls for the long term. He

certainly hadn't planned to meet her. He had simply planned to get absolutely shitfaced out of both joy (his birthday) and sorrow (his separation).

The morning after what should have been nothing more than a drunken one-night stand, on Saturday around noon, she awoke and toked up to burn off her hangover. He opened his eyes. The strange surroundings smacked him in the face: her messy little bedroom with DMB and Guster posters thumbtacked to the wall and curling up at the corners, the Ikea dressers shoddily put together, a twenty-three-year-old chick with the bowl of weed still in her mouth. He hadn't seen something like that in years he said, since college. "Wake 'n' bake, right?" But he was so old he didn't even know the hip term any more.

As they lay in bed smoking weed and having more sex, he told her she was the first girl he'd had sex with since he split with his fiancée. She assumed she'd never hear from him again once he left around 3:00 that afternoon, but then he sent her a fax at work that next Monday. He'd never gotten her cell number, and could only make out the office fax number on her business card he'd spilt beer on. The cover sheet to the fax said: "To whom it may concern that likes what most concerns me. REPLY TO: me and my dick." It was completely ridiculous. She was glad her boss hadn't seen it.

They were soon dating, though that's such a loose term for what they were actually doing. They were not dating like he'd dated his fiancée. He was dating her like a twenty-three-year-old would have dated her. They pranced around town, drinking cheap beer and booze at loud bars until 4 AM. He started dabbling in drugs with her, stuff he hadn't done since college: smoking pot, popping pills, she he even got him to try "Molly" once. He told her it made a Grateful Dead poster on her wall come to life and he tried to give the dancing bears a hug.

He saw her one weekday night a week, one night a weekend. They never once went to sleep without first sleeping together. He was youthful, trim, and had a full head of hair, so it never looked that ridiculous when they gallivanted around her kinds of bars and her kinds of friends. No one ever said, "Why is that *old* guy here?!"

She was youthful though, even for her age, so it *did* look ridiculous when he took her to fancy cocktail lounges and chic hotel bars and she got ID'd. Sometimes the bartenders would ID him too, not because they thought he was too young, but just to learn the age gap for their own amusement.

She was 23, he was 32. Their ages reversed. It's hard to think of numerically reversed ages that would ever not be ridiculous. At worst it would be a May–December romance of criminal proportions. At best, *them*.

When they'd run into his friends at places like Pegu or DBA, they'd be excited to see him and amused to see her on his arm. He didn't care though. He'd never felt better. Not happier, just *better*. He was ignoring happiness in favor of feeling better.

They say you can't recapture youth, but sleeping with a twenty-three-year-old is a pretty good start, he once told her. And they say only age brings wisdom, but sleeping with a thirty-three-year-old was good in that regard as well.

Their days became a whirlwind of late nights and later mornings. In his engaged life, he liked to wake up *not* hungover at 7 AM *at the latest* to get in a morning workout at Equinox. Now, they were on her childish schedule. Sleeping in late and staying in bed later. The recreational alcoholism of youth, low-level drug use, and plenty of rambunctious sex.

He was someone to be both jealous of and pitied. Mocked and admired.

Things change in a hurry. It was easy to see how a life can have so many paths.

He should have been an "old" married guy by his 32nd birthday. An old guy now mocking his perv friend still sleeping with a young chick, parading her around a town she couldn't afford. Instead, he was now the perv and she was his little girlfriend. But, he was the one justifying his ridiculousness, mocking his pathetic married friends to her. Mocking them for being with boring "old" women their own age. *His* own age. Disgusting!

She thought plenty women his age were pretty, despite what he said. He'd totally rail on them, pointing out how they surely had drooping breasts under their clothes, stretch marks on the sides like a deflated balloons, their areolas smearing into the skin, the eraserhead nipples pointing closer to perpendicular than parallel to the ground. He claimed their stomachs were no doubt a doughy mess from late-night ice cream binges, their new-found self-identification as "foodies" just an excuse for having become "fatties." He could be cruel! He guaranteed their asses looked like a hunter had accidentally nailed them with buckshot. So much cellulite and pock marks you'd look for the nearest caulk gun to fill it all in.

His rants scared her, even though she didn't believe such destruction could happen to the female form in just a decade. But she never forgot his words and always prepared for the future, treating her young body and mind with respect for old age. That's the thing she most learned from him.

"Enjoy your youth," he'd note. "It goes by in a hurry."

Still, she could tell from his voice that he sadly longed for these "old" women his own age. She knew he didn't truly find them disgusting. She thought he actually found himself disgusting for fucking her.

But she got things from his year of living ridiculously too. And not just sexual experience. She got wisdom and happiness and trips to restaurants she could have never afforded at that age. She got knowledge of New York City's intricacies that would have taken years to develop. He was her shortcut to a true, ridiculous adulthood.

Then, at his 33rd birthday party, exactly one year after it had started, it ended. She was obviously not important enough to him to have a romantic birthday dinner at Daniel—nor could she afford the tab—so instead he thought it would be fun to invite all his stuffy friends to her favorite shithole bar in the East Village. Surprisingly, most everyone showed up at Doc Watson's, all arriving as if there to rescue him. In retrospect, maybe it was his cry for help.

When his ex-fiancée showed up, she knew his year of being ridiculous was over. They didn't break up that night; they just kind of floated apart like deflating balloons. They didn't even mention it; they just Irish goodbye'd an entire relationship.

But she wasn't mad.

She was me.

🏷 **Perdition** (w. 49th St. and Tenth Ave.) | 12:29 AM

chapter twenty-one
THE GIRL WITH THE DRAGGED-ON TABOO

"Ollie ended up getting re-engaged to that same woman a few months later. And now I'm almost his age…"

"You ready to get ridiculous?"

"I just might be."

"I never knew Ollie was so…old! I just thought he was boring."

"Yeah, well, I've learned there are really only two ages of men."

"What?" Erin wondered.

"Single. And not."

We had escaped to a spot called Perdition. It was so dark you could barely see an inch in front of yourself. Trying to order drinks, I slipped beside two douchebags sipping Amstel Lights, the buzzwords "price point" and "platform" popping up several times as I approached. As I hit the bar their conversation ceased, and I noticed them both subtly trying to ogle me. I saw the gears slowly churning in their brains as they tried to think of some interesting opener, like that would actually matter. Unless you wanted to be flirted with by losers, getting drinks at a bar had to be a smash and grab job. Unfortunately, the bartender wasn't making it easy for me.

She was clad in a tight black tank top barely preventing her boobs from spilling out, slowly shaking a cocktail as she consulted an iPad. Female bartenders were the worst and as a feminist, that was hard for me to admit. If you asked them for anything other than a beer or a (blank) and (blank) they were often clueless. "An old-fashioned…what?!" they might say, before walking over to a male cohort, or the bar's iPad, to Google what was in such a cocktail.

"Do you know what Perdition means?"

I turned my attention from the ass-dragging bartender to the asses beside me.

"Perdition?"

Both men smarmily smiled. Of course, if they had been cuter, a dumb opening line wouldn't have mattered. Us women had such awful double standards like that. We were only feminists when it was convenient. Just then, Erin cut in.

"Perdition. P-E-R-D-I-T-I-O-N. The final state of damnation. 'Hey Cheryl, these dudes beside us are surely in a state of pussyless perdition what with their lame pick-up lines.'" She looked annoyed, turning toward the bartender now leaning on the bar faux-dreamily, as if posing for a glamour shot, pretending to care about a boring conversation with the douches she'd just made a drink for. "Hey Boobs McGee, can we get some drinks?!"

The bartender looked perturbed and so did the customers trying to over-tip their way into her bar apron.

"Yeah?"

"Two beers. In two glasses."

I had to laugh at the modern state of feminism. Some people might see a bartender with her boobs hanging out, in full control of the slobbering crowds around her, as a powerful women. Others might see Erin as one for swatting down such perceived misogyny. But, the fact of the matter was, women were a slight majority in the world—and despite the name, a fairly big one in Manhattan—and we had more control over our destinies than we appreciated.

"CHERYL??!!!"

Surprised by hearing my name, I turned to see an old co-worker I could barely remember.

"A...NNETTE!!!??"

There's no more shrill a noise than the one made by two women who haven't seen each other in awhile.

"I haven't seen you since...?"

"That dinner party at Amanda's."

"How are you?"

"Not bad. Still with Fenwick?"

"I am."

"Wow. You must be...an account head by now."

"Creative director."

"Married?"

She held up her ring finger, showing off a sparkling rock that suddenly made Perdition seem not so dark.

"Next month."

"Congrats."

"And you...?"

"Not quite. But I've been...close."

"We all have. Had."

There was an awkward pause as Annette looked down at her engagement ring and I bit my lip.

"This is my good friend Erin."

"Erin! Great to meet you! If you're not here with any one else, get your drinks and join us in the back."

Erin and I glanced toward a back area where some pink helium balloons floated on strings.

"Bachelorette party?"

"Do you see any novelty penises?" Annette joked as she grabbed my hand. "A friend just ended a job. We're celebrating."

We headed toward the back room.

"'Ended'? You mean 'left'? Oh, was she laid off?"

"Neither. More like..." Annette turned over her shoulder and smiled at us. "Laid. Then left off."

We were led to a horseshoe of comfy couches and introductions were made. One of the women—a pretty, pretty, tiny, tiny blonde blonde named Ash—was slugging champagne like it was New Year's.

"God, he was in AA."

"That mattered?"

"Yeah. I wasn't allowed to drink either."

"Sounds rough."

"It was tough."

"Still, another one bites the dust, girl."

I was confused as to what these women were talking about.

"Ash, Annette said you just left your job, but what exactly do you do for a living?"

The celebration and conversation stopped for a second, like I'd made a major faux pas.

"I mean…what did you do?" I tried to pull my foot out of my mouth, not even sure how it got in there in the first place. I inadvertently just jammed it up even further. "I mean…what are we celebrating?"

Ash, in a very friendly tone, responded: "I rarely talk about my job."

Her friends tittered amongst themselves.

"Hey, we all have boring jobs. Yet we still manage to talk about them—mainly to bitch. And, you get to celebrate! You just left such a job, think about that!"

Ash remained somewhat aloof toward me, seemingly tired of having to discuss these things with a stranger.

"Yes. But my career remains the same. And, I never said my job was boring. It's quite interesting in fact. So interesting…you might be repulsed."

Erin and I scooted to the edge of our seats, leaning in toward Ash, our eyes bulging wide.

"Now I truly am interested! What do you do?"

Ash and Annette's other friends looked surprised by my aggressiveness.

"I'm…insurance."

That didn't sound all that interesting.

"Like…what kind of insurance? Health care?"

"I didn't say I worked in insurance. I said I am insurance. Though, it is for people's health."

Now I was really confused and had to push even harder.

"You're with women, many of us drunk. Spit it out, girl!"

Ash looked around, making sure no one could hear her. The rest of the group looked on, as if a great secret was about to be revealed to me and they weren't sure whether I deserved to even know it.

"I'm insurance against loss."

"Yes…?"

"Loss of a relationship."

"But…how do you insure that?"

Ash smiled all-knowingly.

"If a man gets dumped by his girlfriend, or fiancée, and he has a policy with my company, he gets me to replace her." I laughed, still not quite understanding the implications.

"What do you mean?"

She slowly continued. "Let's just say I replace the things a man loses in a breakup."

"Yes…?"

"I am a companion, first and foremost."

"Go on…"

"You get dumped and sure that's awful, but losing the girl pales in comparison to trying to fill your time. Whereas the man used to always have plans, always have somewhere to be, and always have someone to be with, now—*POOF!*—he has none."

"Unless…"

"Unless…he has insurance. Unless he has me."

"You?"

"I help him stay on track, without missing a beat, so he still has a life every single night during this first tough period where most men are a wreck. Drinking like shit, eating like shit, flailing at women."

"Like shit," added one of Ash's friends as they all laughed.

"Beer, buffalo wings, video games, and skanks, right?" added another.

Erin nervously laughed.

"So you're, like, an escort?"

"Hardly."

"But what about…you know?"

"Sexual intercourse?" she said in a mocking tone.

"Yes."

"I'll fuck him if that's part of his policy. I simply replace the sex that has been lost due to his ex's departure. If he was getting it every night during the height of his previous relationship, then so am I giving it to him every night."

She spoke in such a matter-of-fact tone it was hard to think her behavior was anything but normal.

"But I'm not there to be his blank canvas. He's not allowed to experiment with me, to do things he's never done before. He's just using me to…maintain."

"Maintain an erection!" Annette blurted out.

"I'm there to wean him back to singledom."

"Weaning a bunch wienies!" someone else shouted.

"But…how do you live with that?" I wondered, my voice casting more judgment than I wanted it to.

"Very wealthily!"

"But you're a…prostitute!" Erin said, in a voice casting as much judgment as she meant it to.

"I'm not. I'm a healer. No one criticizes doctors for putting their hands on a stranger's body parts to make them feel better. No one criticizes a psychiatrist for having incredibly intimate conversations. Nor do I think I should be criticized for doing those same exact things."

"But isn't it weird to just be assigned some…random dude?"

"We don't choose who we get to touch in this life."

"Do you have a life of your own?"

"By 'life of my own,' I assume you mean do I go home at night, pet a cat, cook some spaghetti, chat with these girls on the phone, update my Facebook page, and then watch some shitty reality TV show about cupcakes? No. I don't do that. Unless he does. But I do have a life of my own. I'm just like a Broadway actress, constantly playing new parts to make people smile. You'd never ask Patti LuPone if she has a life of her own."

"How long does this last?"

"Depends. Some gigs are a mere thirty days. Others—like, for men coming out of decades-long relationships—can extend a full six months. Though they can cancel at any time. If they truly feel healed. If they meet someone new."

"Do they ever?"

"No!" Ash laughed for the first time at the absurdity of it all. "Most just fall in love with me."

We all laughed. Ash explained the next day she was set to move into what she described as, essentially, an upscale sorority house where she would live with other insurance men and women currently waiting for their next gig.

As we finished our one drink and left the group, Erin leaned in toward Ash, handing her a business card. "Let me know if some guy named Joe Waverly ever comes by…"

I wondered how long Ash could possibly be insurance. Was it a lifetime gig? What if she fell in love with someone? She didn't seem like the type, but all girls are the type to fall in love. One day.

Back on the street, Erin shook her head, still somewhat enamored.

"Now that's an empowered woman!"

"I'm not so sure…"

"God, Cheryl, I wonder if she dreamed of that life when she was a little girl?"

"As little girls we rarely dream of what our lives might actually look like."

It was finally time to tell my best friend about my dreams as a little girl finally coming true.

chapter twenty-two

SPEC

```
          "THE MAN OF MY DREAMS" - PILOT

    created and written by Cheryl Sheffield

             © 2013 WGAe Registered


FADE IN:

INT. KAT'S BEDROOM - DAY (1989)

Somewhere in the suburbs.  A pink bedroom
decorated with New Kids on the Block post-
ers, stuffed animals, and photo collages.
KAT (10) sits alone in her bedroom, play-
ing with Barbie and Ken dolls, acting out
a scene between them.

                    "BARBIE"
          Oh, Ken, I'm so lucky to have you.
```

                    "KEN"
        I'm so lucky to have you, Barbie.

                   "BARBIE"
        But what about our friend Kat—
        don't you feel bad for her?

Kat tilts Barbie and Ken so that they look
up at her.

                    "KEN"
        Why is that?

                   "BARBIE"
        Because none of the boys at school
        will talk to her.

                    "KEN"
        Why not? She's so pretty.

Kat smiles sadly.

                   "BARBIE"
        She has braces though. None of
        the boys want to talk to her. She
        wonders when she will ever get her
        first kiss.

                    "KEN"
        I'm sure it will come soon.

                   "BARBIE"
        But from who?
        (corrects herself)
        Whom?

> "KEN"
> Hopefully from her dream man.

> "BARBIE"
> How will we know. What will he look like?

Kat closes her eyes and dreams.

> KAT
> He's tall and strong. He's got spiky hair like Jordan Knight. He's smart, but not a dweeb. He's funny, but not a class clown. He's good at sports but doesn't have to be Michael Jordan. Oh, he's a great dresser. Benneton and Umbro and Structure. But most of all, he just wants to give me a French kiss.

Kat squeezes her Barbie and Ken dolls to her chest and then opens her eyes.

She immediately jumps back out of sheer fright before relaxing, and smiling.

Finally, we see what she sees:

There, sitting on the edge of her pink, lacy, canopy bed is…

THE MAN OF HER DREAMS—

Looking exactly as Kat just described him.

CUT TO:

INT. KAT'S APARTMENT - NIGHT (2014)

A hip one-bedroom apartment in Manhattan's East Village.

Kat, now a gorgeous 32-year-old in a sexy outfit, puts the finishing touches on her makeup while talking to a friend on speaker phone.

                FRIEND (O.S.)
So tell me about this new guy, Kat.

                KAT
(smiles)
Well…his name's Jeff and he's a few years older than us. He's from Scarsdale and he works for a hedge fund. He lives in a stunning highrise off the park…

                FRIEND (O.S.)
Ooooh…have you been back there yet?

                KAT
No. Not yet. But hopefully tonight is the night.

                FRIEND (O.S.)
Naughty girl.

                KAT
Yeah…

Kat grabs some condoms from her bureau and examines them.

>   FRIEND (O.S.)
>   What's wrong, hon? You don't
>   sound that excited.

>   KAT
>   Yeah, well…you know how I have
>   certain…hold-ups.

Kat grimaces and turns—and there, sitting on the edge of Kat's bathtub, is The Man of Her Dreams. Still looking EXACTLY like he looked in 1989—some 1980s-era 10-year-old's dream hunk.

>   T.M.O.H.D.
>   That's what I am now, baby? A
>   "hold-up"? Don't you tell your
>   friends about me? I've been lis-
>   tening to your chats with Erin for
>   over a decade.

Kat quickly mutes her phone to yell at him.

>   KAT
>   Please! What do I have to do to
>   get you out of my life? I'm beg-
>   ging you. I just want some free-
>   dom so I can fall in love with a
>   normal man, with nothing stopping
>   me.

TMOHD smiles widely.

> T.M.O.H.D.
> But I'm not stopping you, baby.
> Why I'm the man of your dreams!
> Remember?

END COLD OPEN.

CREDIT SEQUENCE:

A series of scenes (from the upcoming season) in which Kat struggles to date in New York City with an imaginary (yet somehow tangible) "dream man" always in her way and unwittingly thwarting all her attempts at finding love.

FADE TO COMMERCIAL.

On the Rocks (W. 49th St. and Tenth Ave.) | 1:01 AM

chapter twenty-three
CONTEXTUAL

"Oh my god, Cher! That sounds hilarious."

"Eh, it's kind of a sellout."

"No. Don't say that."

"Well…it's not quite what I'd prefer to do, but the networks like schlock like that."

"No, it's sounds awesome. I want to watch that show, like, right now. Why didn't you tell me about this?!"

I shrugged. I'd been having trouble revealing myself lately. We sat at On the Rocks, a whiskey lounge where most connoisseurs got their drinks neat.

"I guess I'm still coming to grips with having to move out to LA."

"When would you have to go?"

"They want to start pre-production on June 1."

Erin tilted her barstool toward mine and hugged me.

"You finally did it, honey. I'm so proud of you!"

"I haven't done anything yet. Only like 10% of pilots even get picked up so I'm sure I'll be that other 90%."

"Don't be modest. And we've been wasting this whole night worrying about me and my stupid boy problems? We should have been celebrating you. *Now* it's your night! Should we have some champagne?"

As Erin reached into her purse to get her credit card, her phone lit up with a text, making her cavernous purse look like a tiny gold miner was inside.

"Oh, that might be Les!"

And with that she had instantly forgotten about feting me. Wordlessly, Erin turned her phone to show me her illuminated screen:

lol

It was from Joe, listed as "The X" in her phone's contact info. We stared at it for a good minute.

"What does it mean?"

"Maybe he accidentally wrote it."

"Why?"

"He's probably drunk."

Erin grinned stupidly. "Then he's drunk and thinking about *me*."

"Maybe it was meant for someone else. Or it's a typo." I was grasping at straws. "Look, Erin. It's late, he's drunk, and he's lonely. He's trying to goad you into responding."

"Why?"

"He wants to hear from you. So here he's trying to force the issue by screwing with your mind. A decade ago he would have called your landline and hung up before you answered it but just in time for you to see the caller ID."

Erin thought about it for a second.

"So what should I write back?"

"*Should* you write back?"

"I have to."

"Why?"

"I need to know."

She punched something into her phone.

Aaron Goldfarb | 127

?

"How 'bout that?"

I wasn't going to convince her otherwise.

"Fine."

Send.

"I wonder *what* he'll write back?!"

"You're acting crazy."

"He's the one who sent an ambiguous text! You want to hear *crazy*, I should tell you what I've been thinking about doing."

Erin awkwardly turned her barstool toward me. Her drunkenness was starting to show.

"So Joe's favorite restaurant is this burger joint by him in Williamsburg, right? Safari it's called. Their gimmick is selling burgers not made of cows. They have buffalo, ostrich, kangaroo. Pretty much any meat allowed in America, Safari will slap between two buns. Joe likes this stupid place for some reason."

"All men like those kinds of places. Makes men feel more… manly."

"You're right! Joe once said, 'Every time I swallow I feel like I'm digesting a part of the animal's soul.'"

"Weird."

"Gross. Joe goes like once a week. So I was thinking…what if I went on Match or OKCupid or Flakr—that's a new one… you ever use it?"

"Hmmm…"

"And every day for a week, I set up a first date with a *super* hot guy at Safari."

"And…?"

"Well…" Erin smiled at me. "Perhaps I'd coincidentally be on a first date when Joe next arrived. Laughing, joking…maybe the hot guy's touching my forearm and giving me eyes."

"Or stuffing ground lion in your face."

"Well lion's probably not allowed. But do you think that would work?"

"I think it would make Joe pissed. There's certain ethics at play, Erin. When you break up with someone, their favorite restaurant is now off limits!"

"I thought there were no rules in love and war?"

"This isn't love. This is a breakup. That you instigated."

Erin looked bummed as we had a moment of silence, still sitting shiva over the death of her relationship. Just then, she got another text:

XXX

"Now what does that mean?" I wondered. Shit, the bastard had now dragged me into his little game.

"It means he wants to kiss me."

"No. Xs are hugs. An X looks like two arms crossing behind someone's back."

"That's what an O looks like. An X looks like pursed lips. Xs are kisses."

"An O looks like how you form your lips for a kiss. See?" I puckered my lips. "Os are kisses." I put my arms around her. "Xs are hugs."

I nudged the guy sitting beside me, snatching Erin's phone and holding it in front of the man's face.

"Excuse me, what do you think this means…?

He studied the text for a second before looking back at Erin and me.

"It means 'The X' wants to get triple-X with you. *Pornographic*." He looked at Erin and smiled creepily. "Way to go."

I grabbed Erin's phone and turned back toward her.

"Yeah, you're not writing any more."

I grabbed her phone.

"I'm holding this for awhile."

"Everything in New York is too complicated. I should have just married Geoff."

The champagne was going to Erin's head. It was going to mine too, but I had nothing to complain about.

"Who?!"

"You remember Geoff—he visited our dorm freshman year."

"Your high school boyfriend?! From Illinois?"

"Yeah. Geoff. What was wrong with him?"

Let's see…he was a boring, unmotivated hick with a stupid spelling of a common name.

"Nothing. Except he was your high school boyfriend from Illinois."

"So what? Now he's a father of multiples."

"You can't marry your high school boyfriend."

"*Sweetheart*. He was my high school sweetheart."

"There'd be nothing sweet about your life together in… where does he live."

"I think he lives in Libertyville."

"That's really a town name out there?"

"It is! And now Geoff and his wife have everything I waste nights like these trying to find."

"You know what Einstein said: "Marriage is the unsuccessful attempt to make something lasting out of an incident.""

"Yeah, well, I bet even he got married."

She had me there. He had indeed been married. To a woman he hated, cheated on, and eventually divorced, but still… they'd had a cocktail hour and reception at one time I would have bet.

"You sound so anti-marriage, Cher. What's gotten into you?"

"Nothing. In fact, I'm more *pro*-marriage now than I've even been in my life. I'm just pro-getting married the right way."

"What's the 'right way'? Why can't that be with your high school sweetheart?"

I didn't want to be crass like those men who always reminded their buddies getting married, "You're only gonna have one *pussy* for the rest of your life," so instead I asked: "What was your favorite meal when you were fourteen?"

"Random."

"Just answer."

"I was from a small town in southern Illinois. We didn't exactly have fine cuisine. My favorite food growing up was the spinach dip at Ruby Tuesday's."

"And you probably couldn't imagine any food ever being better. Guess what? Then you grew up, went to college, moved to New York and found better food. You then met all sorts of other people who, at one time, also probably thought Ruby Tuesday's spinach dip was as good as it got. Or, a Kraft Singles grilled cheese. Or maybe a Wendy's double cheeseburger."

"Now I'm hungry." Erin grabbed the bar snacks menu.

"By now you surely realize you were wrong about the spinach dip. Marrying your high school sweetheart shows a total lack of courage toward throwing yourself head first into this exciting world and discovering better things. Not to mention: if you'd married Geoff, you would have never met me."

"True."

"But we can't be like men either. Men believe concepts of 'The One' are foolish. They're also wrong. They say stuff like, 'On a planet of seven billion people, how will I ever find just one woman for me?' That's just them justifying screwing as many chicks as possible. Same with whenever they try to bring up science. 'I'm meant to spread my seed!' They always say that: 'spread my seed.' Gross. Luckily, us women are better at recognizing when we've found someone perfect. Men are too concerned about 'What else?' We know the real question should be: 'What more could I possibly need?'"

"Well I know what I need: to find a husband ASAP. We're getting old, Cher."

"How about, instead of asking yourself: who am I gonna spend the rest of my life with? Perhaps you should ask: who am I gonna spend the next year with? Or, this next month? This next week? *Tonight…?*"

"You think?"

"That's the way men think. And look at them! They're all happier than we are."

"Isn't that because they only care about living in the moment?"

Aaron Goldfarb | 131

"Then maybe we should too. Instead, we're dummies who think in reverse. We try to find a life partner and then work backward to the present. Men try to find a night partner and work forward to a life lived happily ever after. We all know Rome wasn't built in a day, yet we all try to find a man we could die with in a day."

Almost right on cue, Erin got another text message.

"If he's trying to triple-X me again, I'll...*show me*."

I too assumed Joe had somehow gotten through the block caller I'd subtly set up. But he hadn't. I held the phone up so Erin could see the text message from Les:

48th & 10th at 1:31? ;)

chapter twenty-four

SLEEPING WITH HIM WHILE HE'S SLEEPING

Unlike Joe's, we didn't critically analyze Les's text. Not even the winking emoticon. (Erin, amazingly, thought it was "sweet," but whatever.) Instead, we dutifully headed to corner of 48th and Tenth, right in front of a Sleepy's mattress store.

"I wondered why he picked this corner, Cher."

"What do you mean?"

"Like…I wonder if he's trying to send me a subtle message."

"A subtle message?" She was sounding drunk.

"Like…" She nodded toward the mattress store. "Start thinking about *beds*. Guys have weird strategies, you know."

"Oh, I know."

"Why is that, Cher?"

"Because guys just don't understand how we work. Or, *what* works."

We stood in silence for a bit, just thinking.

They say men think about sex every seven seconds. That they're always thinking with their brain "down there." That wasn't true for women. When I wasn't having sex, sex was the last thing on my mind. I never thought with my vagina. Except…well, ever since I'd been with *him*.

I, again, checked my phone to see if he had texted me. He hadn't. I had to admit I was getting a little bummed.

When I wasn't with him, all I could think about was sex! *With him*. Looking into Sleepy's, I could see the exact same mattress he had (Sealy Comfort Balance – Queen, $429.99). It immediately made me so horny. God, I couldn't wait to see him tonight. To get in bed with him tonight.

Last night had been so good. We'd been at a new bistro having a delicious meal, but all I could think was: "Can we get through these entrees so I can get home to dessert?!" Even in my head I'd started talking like a porn star. When we got home, and he casually went to the fridge for a beer, just slowing down our process to the bedroom, I knew I had to take charge. So I went down on him right in the kitchen!

Who was I? What had I become? I didn't even really like blowjobs. Who would?! They're disgusting. In theory. But, with him I had become a magnet compelled to his dick. I was so wet. So turned on. I looked up at him from my kneeling position on the ground.

"Are we gonna have sex?" I asked like a unsure teenager.

He just nodded, grabbed his beer off the kitchen counter and took a sip. And then I stripped down so fast you would have thought my clothes were on fire.

Stop, drop, and roll in the hay.

He conked out immediately afterward. Of course he did. Guys always do. But I couldn't fall asleep.

Just last night, I was looking at him sleeping so peacefully on that very mattress. I thought at that moment, still sweaty and spent from sex, staring at his hair falling over his forehead, that it showed such great trust to sleep with someone. I didn't mean great trust as in letting someone put their body inside of yours—or vice versa, although it did—I meant trust as in simply sleeping *next* to someone.

I could kill him if I had wanted to!

I was awake, he wasn't.

I was soberish, he was passed out drunk.

I could have just reached over and squeezed his nose shut, stuck my fist down his windpipe.

Or, I could have taken one of the decorative pillows I'd bought him for some stupid reason—the ones he hated having to deal with every single night and always threw on the floor—and just shoved it over his face!

I could drop rat poison subtly down his throat. Or, prick him with a syringe full of air and plunge. I could slice his throat with any of the gorgeous Kershaw knives I'd gotten him as a Valentine's Day gift.

Or, I could just kick those fragrant bedside candles off the nightstand and onto the highly flammable West Elm rug I helped him pick out during a recent shopping trip to SoHo and light the entire place on fire.

I looked at him sleeping so peacefully, surely exhausted from the remarkable *sleeping-together* we'd just had. (Oddly, our favorite sleeping positions and favorite sleeping-together positions weren't that different: spooning.) Looking at him, so peaceful, I thought: I could easily kill him. Except: I loved him so much.

I'd never let anything happen to him. I'd jump in front of an assassin's bullet to save him. Throw my body in the way of an out-of-control train to prevent his death. Run into a burning building to rescue him.

I loved him so much.

He couldn't die before me.

That was always the final thing I told him before we went to bed.

"Goodnight, Sweetie. I'll love you 'til the day you die."

Even though I said this every night, he still always joked:

"What if I die before you?"

"You won't."

"Why?"

"Because you're not allowed to."

Erin looked at me.

"What's that goofy smile on your face?"

"Oh…nothing. Just enjoying the night."
"Me too."
"And missing…*him*."
"Well is he ever going to meet up with us? I want to see this guy?"

I smiled. He had finally texted me:

C U soon.

"Soon, I think."
And then he'd hopefully take me away from this night of bar hopping.
"Good. Hey, remember that dump?"
Erin nodded across the street toward a place called Sandbar. A douchey joint we used to go to back when we were younger. It was surely the only bar in America with a shoe-check. Sandbar claimed they carted in several tons of "fresh Caribbean sand" every single Monday morning to dump all over the floor. It kinda worked. With its sand floors, warm air, and frozen drinks, Sandbar was the rare tiki lounge that actually made you feel like you weren't in New York. That was, until you saw dorks in blazers on the dance sand.

Erin looked back at me mischievously and now nodded toward the mattress store.

"I can't believe I'm saying it…but I think it actually worked."
"What?"
"Well…standing by all these mattresses is making me kinda, like, want to have sex. With Les. *Tonight*."
"Are you actually attracted to him?"
"Something like that."
"Really? How…something? Isn't he a little…out of your league?"
"Cheryl!"
"I meant the wrong way."
"Maybe."
"He's pretty nerdy."

"But he fits my criteria."

"What?"

We glanced across the street as some drunk bro was tossed from Sandbar. The drunk bro threw his shoes at the bouncer's head. The bouncer ducked out of the way and then chased the barefoot man down the street.

"His shoes."

"Yeah, I saw."

"No. I mean *his* shoes. Les's. You can tell a lot by a man's shoes."

"That's the dumbest thing I've ever heard."

I looked at all the barefoot men and women smoking in front of Sandbar. Their disgusting feet standing on the dirty pavement. How did that bar pass NYC Health Code? It had an "A" right on the window.

"But it's not."

"I would think all you could tell is how much money he spends. On shoes. Or whether he just walked through some dog crap in Central Park."

"Oh no—you can tell so much more."

"Like what?"

It was no wonder Erin always ended up unhappy when she lived her life with such stupid criteria.

"Well…men who always wear sneakers are children. Once you're out of college, the only place a man should wear sneakers to is the gym. All the worse if they're high-tops. Even more so if they're pricey, like new Air Jordans or something he had to wait in line for. You can quickly tell this man doesn't make good financial decisions."

I laughed.

"To a lesser extent, you have a man in Chucks…"

"Ooh, I kinda like the Converse look."

"You like skinny, bearded hipsters?"

"Sometimes. Why do hipsters get such a bad rap?"

"Because they deserve it. I like a man I could believe would actually have a 401k sometime in our lifetime."

"Tough economy. So, what, you want dress shoes all the time?"

"Of course not. If you're still wearing dress shoes and you're not at work, you must have a real stick up your ass. You need to change before you leave the office."

"Sounds like you want Mr. Rogers."

"No. But it reminds me of those women riding the subway in business suits while wearing bright white New Balance. Now *they*'ve clearly given up."

"Not even a wedding ring is a clearer sign a woman's taken. A woman who wants to actually attract men would never dress like that."

"Cheryl," she was slurring a bit. "I just like a man that is a man. Who has some money, has some style, some originality. Cleanliness. Has a good heart."

"Toms."

"Yuck. You can buy those at the supermarket. Both me and a poor girl in Africa don't want to date him."

"Flip flops?"

"Are you kidding me, Cher?! Maybe if I wanted some surfer dude. That's totally unacceptable for an adult in New York."

"How about boots? Rugged, manly…"

"Manly is fine, rugged is not. We live in a cement jungle."

"You're classist."

"Am not. I just want a man with class."

"Loafers?"

Erin finally smiled, thinking to herself.

"Mmmm…maybe."

"Sockless."

I smiled as her expression turned sour.

"Gross. WASP city. Nantucket reds, a belt with whales on it, tousled hair. Yuck."

I spied a scruffy guy in a black leather jacket enter Sandbar.

"Zippered."

"Eurotrash."

"Then how 'bout some sensible, comfortable, tan walking

shoes? From Rockport."

"Hello, grandpa. Nice toupée."

"Probably rich though."

"That's not *all* I care about."

"Velcro."

"Moron."

"Me?"

"Him."

"Then what? You've exhausted everything, Erin. What shoes is a man allowed to wear in order to get to have sex with you?!"

Just then, we heard a loud whistle. I assumed Erin and I were being drunkenly catcalled until we turned toward the whistle, just in time to see Devin and Les having exited Sandbar. There was a goofy smile on Les's face that he struggled to contain as he slipped on his shoes. Devin shook some sand from his sneakers before putting them back on.

"Speak of the devil," Erin quietly said, smiling across the street and toward Les.

"The devil in the fuckable shoes?"

"Why were they at that douche dump?"

"Seeing if they had any better options than these two old ladies?"

"We're not that old."

Once the two boys crossed the avenue and reached us, we began walking north and up the slight Tenth Avenue incline into the dark Hell's Kitchen abyss of the upper 50s.

"Nice shoes, Devin. You like those, Erin?"

She looked down toward his beat-up Nike low-tops and rolled her eyes.

"Well what about mine?"

Les lifted up his foot and Erin smiled.

"Nice. *Very* nice."

Driving shoes?! I glared at Erin.

"What? Like you're some dating expert," she whispered back at me.

"Well I used to be…" I mumbled under my breath.

chapter twenty-five
THE EXPERTS

NerveCenter HQ looked like one of those "cool" offices featured on some *20/20* segment shot right as the dot-com boom was beginning. A place more fit for Silicon Valley in 1997 than upstate New York in 2004. It was a warehouse loft, high ceilings and exposed pipes, industrial-looking if not for the beautiful parquet floors, the high-end furniture from Nordic designers. There were no personal offices (save one) and no personal cubicles (save the four set aside for "inspirationapping"). Just a bunch of couches and chairs and coffee tables as desks. A bottled water machine and commercial espresso maker and more fountain soda taps than a Wendy's. At 5 PM every day a certain code even allowed employees access to as much draught microbrew as one could drink.

"Cheryl Sheffield here to see—"

"Peter. Take a seat, he'll be ready in a sec."

I wasn't sure why I was all the way up here in Hopewell Junction. Was this a job interview? Back then, I applied to anything, just looking for something to latch onto. In their extremely well air-conditioned waiting area, a pretty desk girl sat playing Minesweeper.

"It's cold in here. The air feels nice."

"Peter believes cold air keeps people more alert. Like at casinos."

From my seat, I could see the entire office, packed with young men and women, not necessarily good-looking but well-put-together, *adult*. Fanned out on a coffee table were a dozen female lifestyle magazines. I picked up a two-month-old issue of *CityGirl* with a cover tease: "The Best Sex Positions For Weight Loss." But, before I had a chance to investigate whether it was legitimate for my thighs to burn after reverse cowgirl, my name was called.

"Cheryl? Peter is ready for you…"

I was ushered into the office of an obese man in worker's coveralls. Later I would learn that, though NerveCenter was clearly a white-collar facility, Peter preferred to think of his business as a down and dirty factory, pumping out ideas like an assembly line. Thus, he dressed like a factory foreman, a funny sight considering he wore a $2500 bespoke suit underneath the coveralls and sat behind a Parnian desk more expensive than any car in the lot.

"Have you Lycos'd us, Cheryl?" He talked in a thick Brooklyn accent that likewise seemed a bit of a put on.

"Not exactly," I replied.

"Do you know what we do here?"

"Not quite."

"That's not a surprise. Most people haven't heard of us. And we don't appear on search engines."

"OK…"

"Basically…we are experts. 'At what?' I'm sure you're going to ask."

"At what?" I asked, playing along.

"What we provide is the expertise that shapes the of-the-moment opinions of countless men's and women's sex and relationship magazine, websites, and journals throughout North America if not, occasionally, the entire world. Though Asia can be a tough market to penetrate. No pun intended."

"I see."

"We are basically the central clearing house that comes up with all the ideas. We determine the current thought on sex and relationships in this world."

"OK."

"So, Cheryl, hon, you got my spiel? Youse ready to moveta' town?"

"Move to town?"

"Yer already here. You could clock-in ASAP. I could getcha some custodial guys to retrieve yer stuff in the city. Start workin' for me today and by the end of yer shift, you'd be already set up with employee housing."

Luckily for Peter, I didn't have much of a life back in New York. I was floundering on the dating scene in New York, still confused how it worked, and how to make it less ridiculous for myself.

"But what about my apartment in the city? I couldn't stick my roommate with an empty room, mate."

"What's the rent on the room? Ten bucks sez it's in Murray Hill."

"It is. $1000 flat for the flat."

Peter started laughing heartily.

"That's so cute! And so is yer wordplay. I'll tell youse what. I'll pick up the rent 'til the end of the year. That way, if you don't like it here, you can quit at the droppa da hat and move back to the Apple."

With such a strong hourly salary and benefits, my own Sony Vaio laptop, plus a free employee house and car, it was an offer nearly impossible to pass on. I gave Peter the keys to mine and Erin's Murray Hill apartment, called her at her office to tell her what I had done, and accepted the job.

"Well…get to work, doll."

I wandered aimlessly around the floor of my new office for a bit. I didn't know the protocol and I didn't want to get in anyone's way. I headed over to the coffee machine and grabbed an iced hazelnut and a cheese Danish. I took my breakfast and sat in an open chair in a cluster of chairs where other NerveCenter employees "worked." Some slept, some stared off into the distance, some goofed around playing Minesweeper, none acknowledged me.

I removed my Moleskine from my bag and uncapped a pen. I labeled the top of the page "IDEAS" and drew a thick line underneath it until I nearly tore through the paper. It was hard to do work when work wasn't assigned to you. To a certain extent, I'd always admired my friends who were pencil pushers. Arrive at work, some boss-type told them to do this, count this, file this, sell this, and they went about doing that. I'm sure they never had any sort of "block" when it came to thinking about producing. There was no such thing as pencil pusher's block. No such thing as bean counter's block. Unfortunately, there was writer's block and it was a lifetime affliction.

Just a few hours earlier I'd still been in the low-paying employ of MetroMetro, producers of those free daily newspapers handed to morning commuters before they boarded their trains, whether those were subways, elevated trains, BART, SEPTA, or the Metro in DC. At MetroMetro I had been responsible for writing 300 words daily about the upcoming day's "coolest" after-work events for the Livingstyle section. That simply entailed a half hour of lazy Yahooing and then a fairly by-the-book piece.

Now I wondered how a writer could come up with ideas about love and sex that would presumably shape the current thought in America if not the world. What responsibility I had! I thought about the recent slut phase I'd gone through. The year of living ridiculously I'd just been freed from by Mr. Brian "Ollie" Oliver. Surely I could use that. That must have been what the other young people did. Draw from their own lives.

Still, I sat there in my big seat, just thinking for the rest of the afternoon. It felt like detention. Gradually, more and more of my new colleagues starting packing up for the day and leaving—not a single one hitting the free beer tap, which *blew my mind*. Soon I was the only one still in the main part of the office. Peter came by to ask how I'd fared.

"I've got nothing so far."

"Relax. Just think about advice that once moved you. Then it'll flow like yer period, honey."

I tried to take that piece of advice to create my own advice, but for the rest of the week, the same thing happened. I'd arrive early, grab a latte and breakfast, and then move to my "favorite" chair. I'd open my Moleskine, rack my brain trying to think of ideas, but none ever came. No one spoke to me, no one ever invited me to lunch, no one offered to take me out drinking after work. I couldn't believe none of the men even tried to hit on me! I was fresh bait! I'd go home at night lonely and cry, watching endless hours of network sitcoms and *Sex and the City* DVDs Erin had sent as a housewarming gift, gorging myself on the free food our refrigerators were stocked with every single week.

The second week at work I decided to just give up and head home if nothing changed by Friday. That's when I finally had my "Aha" moment. I looked around and noticed that when I said "Hi" in the hallways and got no response, it wasn't because my coworkers were jerks, it was because they were nerds.

They didn't ask me to lunch, or to go out drinking, because they were too scared to do such things. They nervously blew by me in the halls, staring at the floor instead of making eye contact. They didn't hit on me because they would have had no clue. The men were scared of the women and the few women were scared of the men.

One afternoon, I drank a few too many free Saranacs and forced my way into a happy hour with the guy who always sat beside me. Jared was kinda cute in a Rivers Cuomo way. I asked him if there was anything to do in Hopewell Junction, and he shyly noted there wasn't, not really, something I had already noticed in my leisurely drives around town. I wondered if he knew a single bar in town because, I told him, I'd love to go out drinking with him.

"I think there's…I mean, I once…I know…I bet the Applebee's off the highway has a bar."

"Then we'll go there."

Jared was tough to get talking early on—he'd clearly never dealt with girls before—but with each additional bottle of Brooklyn Lager he opened up more. He admitted he'd only been working at NerveCenter for a year himself. He noted that no one in the office really talked to each other and no one had friends. He told me Peter was a total pervert who lived in a McMansion with a harem full of hookers and didn't believe or care about any of the hooey we published in our magazines—he only cared about making money. Jared also revealed he was a virgin.

Yes, of course I slept with him that night. I awoke that morning after with a hangover of enlightenment. My head was throbbing but I felt so powerful now that I realized no one at NerveCenter knew anything about sex. In fact, many of my colleagues were just like Jared: young, stupid, clueless, virginal. Just like most young Americans. Young, stupid, clueless, virginal, and grasping at any worthless advice lobbed at them.

It now became very easy to write pieces because it truly didn't matter what I wrote.

What's Your Vagina IQ? (CityGirl)
How to Choreograph the Motion of Your Ocean (Cosmo)
Love at First…Smell? (RedBook)

It was all a big fucking joke. The more absurd the joke, the better. It became easy. I cranked out several articles, columns, and sex quizzes per day, all written under different pseudonyms. I was really helping the ad dollars roll in, lining Peter's pocketbook and surely expanding his hooker harem. He rewarded me with bonus after bonus and a few encouraging slaps on the ass too. I was goddamn rich and goddamn miserable. I had to get out.

DOES ANYONE AT WOMEN'S MAGAZINES GET LAID?
A former writer reveals all

I didn't give my two weeks' notice to Peter. I simply skipped town once I'd landed an agent and he had sold that 3000-word exposé to *Playboy*. Under the pseudonym Kat Brown. I was a real wussy back then. Peter, of course, knew it was me and tried to sue for defamation. It didn't work. It was all true.

As the final line of my exposé noted: *My life of expertise was now over, but that didn't mean I couldn't still become an expert.*

● **J. Mac's** (w. 57th St. and Eleventh Ave.) | 1:35 AM

chapter twenty-six

SEX AND/OR THE CITY

"I never knew that's what you were doing upstate!"

"I said I was working at a startup."

"Who knew what that meant back then! I just assumed you were in a cult or something."

"You even read some of my pieces without knowing they were written by me."

"Did I ever follow the advice?"

"Some. But most you thought was bullshit."

"Good." Erin laughed. "I still like to read women's mags though."

I smiled. "You know, I kinda do too…"

Of course, Peter assumed my *Playboy* piece would put an end to his business. It didn't. Some people may have read *Playboy* for the articles, but not many. The people who did believed my exposé, but others still liked reading the slop *CityGirl* put out. The veracity of the content didn't matter, just the amusement it offered.

"But mainly because I now know how the sausage is made."

Devin and Les glanced each other. I thought they were about to make some double entendre sausage joke.

"Has it worked in your own life?" Devin wondered.

"I guess. I do like a hot, *thick* sausage every now and again."

Erin rolled her eyes. We now sat in the disgusting J.Mac's Bar and Grill. It made places like Rudy's and Drunx seems like presidential palaces in the United Arab Emirates.

"So Devin, you've never told us what you do for a living." Erin probed him.

"I guess you could say I'm an entrepreneur."

"Isn't that just—" Erin smirked, "what people who can't work for a boss and don't make any money say?"

Devin smiled knowingly. "Exactly. Les…"

Les handed Devin some bills and Devin promptly headed to the bar. Erin looked at Les.

"Your friend is smarmy."

"I'm not even sure what that means," Les responded, before conceding, "but it's probably true."

Erin slinked out of the booth. "God, I hope this bathroom is clean. I'm too tired and tipsy to hover."

Like a little confused puppy dog, Les watched Erin as she headed off toward the bathroom. I was now alone with him for the first time all night. It was my chance to finally talk to him about anything I wanted to.

"So…?"

Les nervously looked around, pretending to examine a Heineken beer mirror that hadn't been cleaned in years, its grime nearly making it non-reflective.

"So."

Sitting so close to him in the over-lit bar I noticed Les was actually pretty cute. I was growing to like him. He was nerdy, but the fact he was Devin's best friend told me he must be secretly awesome. He was just too smart. Some smart guys were able to use their skills to become master strategists at getting women into bed. Like Devin, it would seem. While others, like Les, had so many thoughts bouncing around their screwy little heads they became flustered and quit. And, just like mainstream TV shows did, just like my agent had pleaded with me to do with my own show, I'd always thought nerdier guys needed to just "dumb it down" for the masses.

"I…liked that experts story of yours. It was a good story."

"Yeah."

"But…like, do you think there is any place men can go to get 'expert' advice?" He used air quotes, which was adorable. "Devin says chick flicks…but, eh, I don't know."

I leaned in toward him, deciding to just go for it. He retracted, thinking I was about to kiss him.

"You know, there *is*. Les, let me tell you something no one else is going to. Certainly not any men. Your buddy Devin is close, but not quite right. But, women won't tell you this either, because they don't realize it and would feel stupid saying it."

Les stared at me with a tilted head, confused like a little puppy dog who had just been yelled at for eating the cat's food.

"It's *Sex and the City*. *Sex and the City* is the one place that offers all the answers both sexes need."

"The…TV show?"

"Well I ain't talking about the movie!"

Up at the bar, struggling to get service, Devin glanced back at Les and I hunched together talking. Did I notice a glint of jealousy in his eyes?

"Les, women would never admit it, they might not even know we do it, and men would surely deride it, but it doesn't matter. All that matters is *that* it matters."

Les nervously laughed.

"You've, uh, watched a lot of it, huh?"

Les looked at me like I was a crazy girl that said crazy things, a religious wackjob in Times Square yelling about abortions and the fiery pits of hell.

"What I'm telling you is this: *Sex and the City* is like a crystal ball for how your relationship is gonna go if you're a man. Especially if you're a man having problems with a woman."

Now Les clearly thought I was spewing Times Square craziness and he quickly glanced back toward Devin at the bar, surely wondering what was taking him so long to return.

Aaron Goldfarb | 149

"*Sex and the City* is an oracle to us women, an oracle that was of modest power when it was airing weekly on HBO, but now that it's on all the time on E! and TBS, and we have all the DVDs, and episodes saved to our DVRs, and we've seen every episode dozens of times…now this oracle is seared into our brains!"

"Could you…explain that more?"

"The show has the unique ability to tell us our future! To tell us whether it's gonna get better. Or worse! If it's gonna work out and lead to marriage, or flounder and lead to the end. Or, neither of those two things and just continuously lead to bed."

Les clearly thought I was drunk. Maybe I was. Would I have been having this rant sober?

"You've thought about this a lot, huh?"

"I have. Ask yourself, Les, what exactly is your current dating problem. And then see how Carrie handled it…"

"Like…?"

"That one guy in the pilot was moving too quickly so Carrie told him to slow it down. Mr. Big was going too slowly in committing, so Carrie said speed it up. He never did so she left him. That guy who does the voiceovers in Applebee's commercials was too nice, so she went back to an asshole. Mr. Big wasn't a big enough asshole, so she went to an even bigger asshole. Baryshnikov was *such* an asshole he took her to Paris where she found herself stranded in a luxury hotel room bitching about her life until Big took her back to New York. Man, she was a rollercoaster ride in high heels, huh?"

Les laughed, though I couldn't tell whether it was at me or with me.

"Unfortunately for you, all girls copy that crazy rollercoaster ride. *Sex and the City* is the ultimate cheat sheet in this regard. I know it's stupid. And, you might not believe me, but trust me. It matters. I'm even aware of this effect, yet it still affects me."

Les finally seemed a bit engrossed.

"But what came first? The issues that *Sex and the City* addressed and analyzed…? Or, did *Sex and the City* both invent the problems and then tell women how to handle them?! It's like…remember when Carrie farted in bed with Big and was so embarrassed. Am I crazy or…?"

Now Les was certainly engaged and off and running with his own thoughts on the show, which he was surprisingly well-versed in. I'd often wondered how long this *Sex and the City* cheat sheet would remain relevant for. The show debuted in 1998 and had now been off the air for over six years. Younger women had probably never even watched it.

The really old episodes that still ran in syndication? Painful! So dated. Carrie talking directly to the camera, all these man-on-the-street interviews, and that stupid character Skipper. Carrie smokes like a chimney, doesn't have a cell phone, doesn't know how to use the internet, and no one has Facebook. A bunch of old ladies, in retrospect, going to nightclubs that probably never even existed, and wouldn't have even allowed these late-thirtysomethings in anyway. I can also tell you, at their age, which I guess is now *my* age, they'd have been way too tired to do that kind of stuff on a weeknight. Then again, I quickly checked my watch…Christ…it was 2:01 AM.

"But, though *Sex and the City* is dated overall, it's not dated on dating. Carrie might not have an iPhone, or have lived through this recession, and she's somehow rich from simply writing a once-a-week column in a little-read free newspaper, but us girls don't care about that. We care about her takes."

"So you're all 'Carrie?' Is that what you're saying?"

"Uhn-uh. Nope. Most women actually compare themselves to Charlotte. She's the most prude and technically the prettiest and certainly the least stupidly dressed."

"Right."

"Some women, the super serious types, compare themselves to Miranda, though never in looks. No one ever says, 'I'm just like Samantha!' No one admits to being a slut, Les. Only chaste attention whores even dress and act like they are."

I'd blown his mind.

"But, the fact of the matter is, we all have a little of each girl in each of us. And to us, Les, you all have a little of the guys in you. Like, you're an Aiden. Honorable, moral, kind."

"Great." He rolled his eyes. "No one likes the 'nice guy.' That's what I've been telling Devin my problem is."

"Just continue being an Aiden and the older you get, the easier it will get."

"What's Devin?"

"Devin is…well…"

"He would have never been a character on that stupid show!" Les cracked. We both laughed. It was probably true.

"What were you two talking about so closely? You were getting animated."

Devin returned, setting a round of sweaty Budweiser longnecks in front of us.

"Oh…not something you need to know about."

Devin sat down beside me for the first time all night. Was he finally making his move?

"You never know."

I accidentally grazed his upper thigh as he smiled at me.

"I *know*."

Erin returned from the bathroom, looking a little confused that the only empty seat was now next to Les, as if we'd intentionally set her up.

"My thighs are burning."

"You had to hover?" Les wondered.

"I had to hover high. For a long time."

"It's dangerous to be a woman, babe."

chapter twenty-seven

THE DANGEROUS LIVES OF WOMEN

Just last week, I sat in the You Enjoy Nail Salon getting a pedi. The woman doing my pedi talked in Vietnamese to the woman beside her who did a pedi for the woman above her, a sixty-something woman who spoke to me in English:

"It can be dangerous to be a woman in this city."

The woman turned the copy of the *New York Post* she was reading to show me a story. A woman in Times Square had been assaulted by a man wearing a Batman costume.

"My mom back home worries about me. She's never lived in a big city, never lived in a…how to put it a little more PC than she would?"

"'Melting pot?'"

"Exactly. She's still stuck with that 1970s notion of New York. Blackouts and riots and the Son of Sam. With muggings, rapings, and perhaps an occasional terrorist attack to boot."

The old lady touched my forearm warmly.

"I still remember, darling."

"My mom wants me to call her when I have to travel late by myself. She encourages me to use cabs over the big, bad, filthy subway. 'I'll pay your fare!' she always says."

"That's sweet. I do that for my kids too."

"But do you send them pepper spray every Valentine's Day? I'm sure that breaks some sort of U.S. postal law."

"Yeah, probably."

We looked down at the heels of our feet being scrubbed with a coarse file as the hot vat of paraffin was prepared.

"If your mom only knew. New York is so great nowadays."

"I love it."

"But it's still dangerous. Not because of muggers and rapers and creeps."

"No?"

"No, it's dangerous because of *this*."

She pointed down at the two Vietnamese women below us.

"Beauty comes with a price!"

Our feet were dipped in the wax, immediately goosing us with an odd mix of pain and pleasure.

"Do you get Brazilians, darling?"

I gave her a curious "how dare you" look.

"No, not *a* Brazilian, *the* Brazilian. I'm not talking about waxing unwanted pubic hair—which does come with some dangers in itself…"

I gave her a curious look, wanting to be anywhere but in the midst of this conversation.

"Yes. When I was younger and still wore bikinis. There was always the potential for bacterial infections."

"Gross."

"But *the* Brazilian is even more pricey—about 200 bucks— and quite dangerous."

"I've heard about it, but what exactly does it do?"

"It's a straightener. You got curly hair. In fact, it'd work perfect for you. Turn it straight and shimmery for months."

"I can't really afford that."

"As I said: Beauty comes with a price."

"What happens?"

The Vietnamese women began plucking the hardened wax from our feet.

"The stylist smooths your hair straight by sealing liquid keratin into it with an iron."

This woman had gorgeous hair, especially for her age. I couldn't deny it.

"The thing is though, a lot of these treatments use formaldehyde."

"Formaldehyde?!"

"Right. So the salon has all this formaldehyde gas floating in the air. Makes me nauseous. It irritates the eyes, blurs your vision. We're all coughing and blowing gunk out of our noses. Our throats getting scratchy. Rashes developing on our foreheads. Everyone getting dizzy. It's like working in a factory. Not to mention the chemicals eventually start seeping into your brain."

"Ugh."

"I'll be dead before it's done any damage, but in thirty or forty years, this city is going to be full of crazy, brain-damaged women."

"Who have beautiful hair?"

"Exactly. Except, their hair will probably have fallen out by then from all this shit."

I laughed. Crazily, *now* I actually wanted the treatment done, having always hated my frizzy hair. I was a smart Ivy League grad, now fully aware of the myriad dangers, and I still wanted it done. Why? Because it would make me look pretty.

We were both lead to the mani table to get our nails done. The woman lowered her voice to a whisper.

"Or look at the world of cut-rate Manhattan nail salons. They say there are only three things in New York that are cheaper than in 'normal' America. Fruit, flowers, and…"

"Mani-pedis?"

"Exactly."

The women began filing our nails, specks of dust flying everywhere.

"There's a nail salon on nearly every corner. Sometimes multiple."

The Vietnamese women suddenly seemed to be listening to us, betraying their feigned lack of English.

"It costs my mom $120 to get her nails done back home. She rarely does it."

"I know. But with cheapness, competition, and speed comes another price…"

The Vietnamese women both quit filing for a split second.

"What?"

"Bacterial, fungal, and viral infections. Hepatitis C, staph infections, warts even!"

One of the Vietnamese women finally spoke up:

"We are licensed and never have problem. You check our Yelp page!"

The older woman shrugged toward me.

"Then forget nail salons. We could talk about Botox and fill-ins, plastic surgery."

"Yeah, I don't exactly do any of those things."

"I didn't do any of those things at your age either. Now I do."

I didn't know what to say.

"But I'm sure you do plenty of other things. You do yoga on a mat you never clean, wear short skirts on a subway bench covered in disease, eat cheap supermarket sushi loaded with mercury. Eyebrow threading, laser face hair removal, tanning in Central Park. Everything us women do to try and attract men is more dangerous than walking in the ghetto at midnight."

I thought about the woman as we walked the dark, but safe, streets of Hell's Kitchen. I was sure gonna miss this city when I left it.

"Forget the dangers of walking the streets late at night. That woman was right. In fifty years the formaldehyde from countless Brazilians will have long seeped into my brain, turning my mind to mush, clogging my follicles so I don't even have the ability to grow any new old lady hair. The Botox in my cheeks and forehead will be getting lumpy, my face looking like Play-Doh. My nails eaten away from infection. Skin destroyed from years of waxing, shaving, and makeup."

"Jesus, Cher."

"Erin, we better be as pretty as we can be now, because we are going to be ugly skeletons one day very soon."

"You look gorgeous, hon."

"So do you."

We playfully kissed each other on the cheeks.

"Well I sure hope chronic masturbation to internet porn has truly turned men blind by the time all this happens!"

Erin glared at Devin's crass barb, increasingly getting annoyed by him. She pulled out her phone, subtly entering his name into Google. She whispered to me:

"See if there are any online mugshots for him."

I smiled as Devin changed the subject.

"Hey, let's get a slice. Couldn't we all use a slice?"

And all was forgotten.

◉ Flaming Saddles (w. 53rd St. and Ninth Ave.) | 2:48 AM

chapter twenty-eight
WHAT MEN WANT

"Cher! He's *rich*."

"You don't know that."

After hitting up Mario's Big Pie for some big slices, we (accidentally) moved to a gay bar down the street, Flaming Saddles. Don't ask. From the outside, it had appeared to be a faux-western saloon and I guess that kind of thing interested Les at this moment in time. Again, I didn't ask.

"That article I found says his company just got $30 million."

"In funding. That doesn't mean he gets the money."

"Still…"

Erin looked up toward the bar where Devin and Les were getting drinks from a shirtless bartender *only* wearing chaps and a ten-gallon hat.

"So you like him now because he's maybe possibly rich?"

"No, I still don't like him. But I'm less annoyed if you like him."

I laughed as we moved to the corner of the saloon. We leaned on the rail of a small padded ring where inside a large, hairy bear in leather rode a bucking pink mechanical bull.

"He's still an asshole, though."

"He isn't to me."

"That's 'cause he wants to hookup with you. But he's an asshole to me. And certainly to his friend Les."

"Maybe Les needs it though. Tough love?"

Erin looked off toward Les.

"Yeah. Maybe." She turned back toward me. "So…? Is your guy ever gonna meet up with us?"

"Yeah. Maybe."

"You ever going to talk about him with me?"

"It's no big deal."

Erin looked around laughing. The big, greasy slice of pizza had clearly sobered her up a bit.

"My point exactly. I'd say it is 'no big deal' because you've had your eyes on that asshole manwhore all night."

"Is *looking* cheating?"

"I wouldn't say that. But I bet your mystery lover wouldn't be thrilled with how much you've been looking."

"It's that noticeable?"

Erin nodded.

"It's kind of sad actually."

Garth Brooks's "Friends in Low Places" played on the bar's video screens. The drunk, gay, and frolicking crowd made the expected snarky comments about its lyrics.

"Sad how?"

"Because you're falling for that same-old misogynist Don Draper bullshit.

Just then, "Cotton-Eyed Joe" picked up on the TV and a massive line-dance of gay dudes broke out. One of them grabbed for our hands and tried to pull us into line with him. I was up for it.

"Let's join them!"

"But I don't know how to…line dance."

"Neither do I!"

We giggled as we attempted the moves, but neither of us could line dance worth a damn. Soon, the gay dudes had quit dancing and surrounded us, applauding and hooting and hollering.

The song ended and we got a few hugs before Devin and Les waved us back over to the bar. They held a giant ski with four shot glasses attached to it, wanting us to join them.

"*What*…is that?"

"Oh god, not a shot-ski."

"A 'shot-ski'? Come on, Cher, it'll be fun."

"You don't say?"

I looked at her and laughed.

The shot glasses were full of cheap tequila.

"One…"

1.5 ounces of hangover in a glass.

"Two…"

All four of us were supposed to simultaneously lift the ski to our face…and chug.

"Go!"

We did. I couldn't believe it. It had actually worked. It was a beautiful display of teamwork. We slammed the ski back on the bar and celebrated with high-fives and hugs all around, in between our winces. Devin even nodded at Erin and she smiled. I guess this was Devin's mea culpa. Or at least his mea drunka. I thought I might yack.

"So where should we end the night, ladies and gent?"

"I don't care, dude," Les noted.

"Then, let's head back to where we started."

"Is that what you want?"

"If that's what you want."

We headed back the few blocks toward Drunx, Erin walking with Les, and Devin walking with me. He put his hand casually on my back, gently pushing me along.

"Devin. What *do* men want?"

Devin looked at me with an intense gaze, and started on one of his trademark soliloquies:

* * *

Cheryl, men want women to like them.

I don't mean they want dozens or hundreds or thousands of women to like them. Of course, that would be great, the ability to pick from thousands. But, all men really want is that one.

You see, most men are not scared of women but of *the* woman. They want to get close to just one woman, but it's far easier to *not* get close to numerous. It was for me when I was younger.

For a man, it can be tougher to have a night of intimate conversation with one woman than it is to walk around the bar having quick chats with dozens of dispensable women.

Don't get me wrong, most men like Les are also scared to walk around the bar having the dozens of approaches and quick chats with strangers, but even for them it's still less nerve-wracking than an intimate conversation with just one woman. Plus, in the former situation, he'll be somewhat drunk. In the latter, not so much.

Now, men will always claim the most important thing for them is "freedom." And women will take that to mean the man is implying he needs the freedom to "banga lotta chicks." He might even think he needs that. For most of my life I thought I did. But, if a man really examines himself, like I finally started do in in my early thirties, he'll see the only reason he actually wants freedom is for the very same reason women do.

Men want to be rich. To impress women.
Men want to be successful. To impress women.
Men want to be famous. To impress women.
Men want to be...*everything*. To impress women.

Men don't really want to be any of these things, so they think. Wasting time working hard, coming up with ideas, spending hours and hours at the office. Being an *entrepreneur*. Who would want that?! But then...why are there rich and successful gay guys? Who are they trying to impress? Surely all they would need in life is to be disease-free and in incredible shape.

Hard work for them, and I guess for us heteros, flies completely in the face of that previously stated idea of "freedom." So, what, you have freedom from one woman "tying you down," except you've got a boss 'n' chain keeping you at the office seventy hours a week? How does that make sense?

If only more men knew the value of those $12 roses you can get at any corner bodega. You don't need to be rich and successful to purchase those. That'll be our little secret, huh, Cher? OK, and, yes, my cover's blown.

Men want pretty women, of course. And any halfway decent-looking woman has had a man stare her in the eyes and say, "You are the prettiest woman in the world."

I'm assuming some women are touched when this happens to them, but in the back of their mind their bullshit detector is also going *way* off. You're thinking…

Either: he's lying to me…

(I swear, he's not!)

Or: he truly believes it and is, thus:

Crazy!

You think, even if I am fairly pretty, I'd have to be delusional to think I'm better looking than Giselle or Scarlett or Heidi. How could I possibly be? They're professionals, whose job it is to look pretty. They have $1000/hour trainers, personal chefs who know how to make them incredibly delicious foods that is somehow non-caloric, not to mention a team of stylists, make-up artists, hair dressers, photographers, and photoshoppers. So, like, no way this man, *my* man, thinks I'm better looking than all them.

But, I swear, he truly does.

If you made him technically analyze the beauty between you and, say, Giselle or Scarlett or Heidi, he wouldn't lie. He'd see their symmetrical faces and flawless bods. He would hesitate before he admitted that, yes, you *aren't* better looking than them. He knows you're not.

But in his eyes…even though they are prettier, he's far more attracted to you. Which makes you the prettiest woman in the world to him.

Men want ease. They don't like people getting on their case. Their whole life has been about people getting on them. Parents and then teachers and coaches and professors and now, we're finally adults, and we don't want a woman who gets on our case too. That's another reason so many men jump from woman to woman. Doing that dilutes the getting-on-our-case-ness.

Men want intelligence. You don't think they do, but they do want women they can discuss real things with. Sure, men like to talk about frivolous things just as much as women do. Sports and beer and dumb TV shows. But they ultimately end up wanting someone who's their intellectual equal.

Men want laughs. A man's entire life would be devoted to laughing if he was able to achieve such a thing. Women often think this means he wants a funny woman. Not true. She doesn't have to be funny. He wants a woman with a sense of humor. A woman that likes to be beside him laughing at things he says or things happening in the world.

A woman's smile, like a genuine, toothy, glistening smile—kinda like you have right now—is sexier to a man than any other body part she could possibly expose. If only women knew how much more value they could get from exposing their teeth than their cleavage.

Men want to take you on dates you enjoy, but they don't want them to be stuffy. Men have no clue though, so they try to emulate what they've seen on TV or read in men's magazines. Men just want a relaxed evening of good food and cheer, nice drinks and laughs. And, yeah, if it ends with sex all the better, and everything prior to that is suddenly irrelevant and we'll gladly do anything and everything you want to get to that endgame.

Men don't need you to do anything crazy in bed. Men just need you to be forthcoming and somewhat uninhibited and kind of know what you're doing. Men just want you to enjoy having sex with them and to tell them how to help you do that.

Men want families. Maybe even with you. Men want children "one day." Maybe even with you. No man really wants a wedding, but most want marriage so they'll eventually put up with the wedding if you want it and as long as your dad is paying for most of it. They'll put up with *how* you want it as well, assuming you let them select the booze.

You women just don't understand what men want.

You think there are so many things men want that you can't provide.

You think you have no chance at giving a man all he wants.

But you do…

You truly do.

We don't want harems or orgies or threesomes or to be dating and sleeping with dozens or hundreds or thousands of women. We don't want to be single for eternity. We don't want to cheat on you. We don't want to grow old by ourselves. We don't want to be playboys or cads or players.

We only choose that life when the option we truly want isn't available.

You see…

Men don't want anything much different from what women want.

We just want the love of one good woman.

As soon as we can get it, for as long as we can have it. Then we'll be happy and content for life.

Well.

That's what this man wants.

◉ Drunx Pub (w. 52ⁿᵈ St. and Eleventh Ave.) | 3:45 AM

chapter twenty-nine
SLUT PHASE

"He said all that, Cher?"

"Yeah. What do you think?"

Erin and I stood in Drunx's empty bathroom, primping in the mirror.

"I think no matter how much I try to cockblock him…it won't matter. You're gonna sleep with him tonight, aren't you?"

"No, that's not what I meant."

After Devin's talk, I couldn't stop smiling like an idiot. His talk had finally convinced me I was giving my man what he wanted.

"I'll admit he is pretty hot. A total jackass who probably sleeps with anything that moves, but he is hot."

"I think Devin might have a softer side than you think."

"And I think all his cares about is showing you his hardest side the second you get back to his apartment."

"Nothing wrong with that."

"You might be right. You know, tonight is starting to feel like we're back in our slut phase from our twenties."

Oddly, it was during that slut phase when I was the most innocent. Fresh-faced, idealistic, optimistic. But stupid. I was

Aaron Goldfarb | 165

mainly a so-called "slut" because my critical thinking skills were lacking.

"I kind of miss that phase."

In our early twenties, going out still meant something to me and Erin. We ritualized it to extreme levels. I thought if I didn't look my best, there was no way I could possibly meet a handsome dude. Of course, now I realize that's terrible thinking. Handsome dudes will sleep with a pretty young thing wearing a Hefty bag.

Back then, we all lived together in Murray Hill. Murray Hell. Saturday nights, Emily, Patti, Danielle, Amber, Hannah, and others would start at our apartment where we'd make a few overly sweet vodka drinks and "pre-game." We only allowed ourselves three drinks at home. We thought that the appropriate number of vodka Ocean Sprays to have in one's system before entering a bar.

We'd drink glass #1 and alternate between heading to the showers and snarking on reality TV (*The Bachelor* was new at the time).

We'd drink glass #2 and take turns working on each other's hair and makeup.

We'd drink glass #3 and begin trying on different shoes with different outfits. Our closets were piled with shoes and we'd wheel rolly suitcases to each other's pads to have even more options. We were stupid enough to think the right pair with the right outfit would land the right man.

I remember this one summer evening. I was so proud of a sexy new pair of Louboutins I had received from my rich grandma as a college graduation gift. Black with a tiny strap, sitting on six-inch heels, my calves had never looked better. And I'd never struggled more to walk. Oh, I was teetering. It's funny us women think high heels make us look so sexy—and they do, when we're standing still. But, the second we try to walk, we're stumbling around like a drunk on stilts.

Saturday nights we'd always head to the strip of Third Avenue haunts directly across from our apartment. Joshua Tree,

Bar 515, Mercury Lounge, it didn't matter, they were all the same. Full of young drunks, a post-graduate bar scene if there ever was one.

Despite my naivety, I always did well with men back then. (I'm not sure that's worth bragging about!) I always drank for free, I always got asked for my number a zillion times per night, I always had the option to go home with many men. Often I did. More often than I probably should have.

Except this one night. I was walking on air, and struggling to walk on the actual ground, but men weren't giving me the time of day. What was up? Yet this one guy Freddie was all over Erin. Nothing makes a young woman more catty than her friend getting the detestable male gaze more than her. It's like that famous line from Gore Vidal: "Every time a friend succeeds—I die a little." Every time a friend gets laid—and I *don't*—I died a little. I'd start bitchily comparing myself to her in my head. I'm prettier. I'm taller. I'm smarter. Though I clearly wasn't if I thought my wits and class mattered more than my tits and ass.

Erin and Freddie were all over each other. Hugging and kissing, all grabby hands and slithering tongues. I grew tired of standing in the corner sucking vodkas through a tiny red straw, and I knew I had to compete with the Joneses by sucking some face. Luckily, Freddie had a roommate, Kevin. Unluckily, he was incredibly ugly. Even less fortunately, I desperately needed to hook up with someone that night to feel good about myself. I couldn't have gone home alone while I knew Erin was having the night of her…well, *night*.

So I accepted his advances and soon the four of us were crammed into the back of a cab heading over the Brooklyn Bridge and into Brooklyn Heights. We arrived at a stunning townhouse with picture windows giving a panoramic view of Manhattan. Freddie was apparently a finance wiz and apparently rolling in it.

"There's the couch—there's the remote—beer's in the fridge—liquor's in the cabinet—pillows sheets towels in the closet good night."

I was confused as Erin and Freddie scurried into his bedroom to hook up. I looked up at Kevin.

"Don't you live here too?"

The answer was no. You see, Kevin wasn't even Freddie's roommate, he was just an unemployed friend crashing on his rich friend's couch as he looked for work. His ugliness suddenly got even uglier.

Within minutes, Erin and Freddie were loudly humping, rocking the entire house. Kevin stared at me and put his hand on my back. Shivers went up my spine as if his hand had some anesthetic on it. He dove in for a kiss and…I let him. He began tonguing me down with a ridiculous force and…I let him. He surely hadn't kissed a girl in ages, perhaps in his life. I let him. The inside of his mouth tasted like a mix of Certs, burnt coffee, and cigarettes. It was like making out with the high school janitor. After all I've told you, what I reveal next won't make much sense but you must remember that, back at this point in my life, I did not cut my losses. Even if I took the wrong fuck in the road I never turned back.

I LET HIM.

He jackhammered me on Freddie's leather sofa, my ass getting burn marks. He threw me around in kama sutra positions he'd probably seen on a dorm room poster. He treated me like an inflatable doll. And…

I let him.

When he was thankfully done, I barrel-rolled off the couch like a suicidal lemming plunging off a cliff, turned my back on him, and tried to pass out, using my new shoes as a pillow.

A couple of hours later, after the worst night's sleep ever, the sun started coming in through those same glorious panoramic windows, scolding me as I slept on the floor. Standing up and staring at the ogre sleeping on the couch, I knew I had to get out of there ASAP. I stood, put my shoes on and went outside without even thinking about my return plan.

My flip phone's battery was dead. I had no cash. At that time, I didn't yet know how the outer-borough subway system even worked. I only had one option: walking. The five miles or so from Brooklyn Heights back to Murray Hill.

Even at 6 AM it was hot as hell out. And the going was slow. North, over the Brooklyn Bridge, from lower Manhattan toward Midtown. My feet swelling because my new and unbroken-in shoes were so damn tight, barely even bending with each step, my toes, feet, heels, and calves burning. It was like the shoes had shrunk over night and my feet had gotten bigger. I was in intense pain.

I will surely be able to handle the pain of childbirth one day as that two-hour, five-mile walk in six-inch heels was pain personified.

Why had I gone home with Kevin? Why had I had sex with him? It wasn't because I liked him.

It was because I didn't like me.

In the early days of your sexual career, especially if you're a girl, you often aren't having sex because you like the guy. You often aren't having sex because you think it will even feel good. You are simply having sex because you like that someone likes you. You like that someone thinks enough of you to want to sleep with you. You even hope it will make someone love you. So worried are you about your place in this world that you sleep with any one just to feel good about yourself.

By the time I walked in the door at around 9 AM, I was a sweaty, stumbling mess. Crying, my eye shadow running down my face, my feet throbbing.

By noon I was laying on the couch watching TV, icing down my bloodied, bruised, and battered feet, and thinking about my terrible night and even worse morning. Then, I saw a candy apple red Porsche pull up in front of our apartment.

Moments later, Erin walked in barefoot, coolly carrying her own heels, grinning ear-to-ear like she'd lost her virginity all over again.

"Why'd you leave so early, Cher? Freddie would have given you a ride. How'd you even get home?"

I could have killed her.

"Freddie's so amazing. He made Belgian waffles for me this morning. Fresh fruit, whipped cream, they were awesome! He's really talented."

I could have slapped her.

"You should have seen his bed. California King, pillow top, silk sheets, sexy canopy. *Unbelievably* comfortable."

I could have punched her.

"Best sex I've ever had! He's like…a magician!"

I could have murdered her.

She sat down on the couch beside me, curiously looking at the floor in front of us, where my shoes rested, the six-inch heels having surely lost an inch from my miserable morning walk.

"By the way…you know you accidentally took my shoes this morning."

I looked down at the floor and what I thought were my shoes. They weren't. I wore a size 9 and those were size 6s. The same brand and style but old and beat up.

"Ha. We have the same red bottoms, Cher. Twinkies."

That was the last time I ever hooked up with someone to make me "feel good" about myself.

My slut phase was officially over.

chapter thirty
THE DAYS OF OUR LOLives

As we exited the bathroom, I noticed three tiny baskets of ransacked complimentary sundries behind the faucets: mints (1/3 full), tampons (fully stocked), and NYC Dept. of Health condoms (only two left). I stuffed some of each into my purse and snuck a condom into Erin's without her noticing.

"So what do you think Les thinks of me?"

"I think he thinks about you what he thinks about *all* girls."

"What's that?"

"That we're scary."

Erin curled her nails toward me.

"RAWR!"

"Why do you ask?"

I looked at her curiously.

"Because, if you're not gonna be a slut tonight, well…I think I am."

I smiled at Erin, my work was finally done for the night. I'd made this single woman happy for at least the next twenty-four hours.

Until she started freaking out in forty-eight hours when Les had yet to make the first post-coitus phone call.

Heading back to our booth to meet up with the guys to call

it a night, we passed three drunken guys swaying and singing along loudly to "Sweet Caroline."

"Les is about to have his mind blown!" Erin smiled at me, raising her eyebrows conspiratorially.

"I can only imagine."

"Cher-uhl! Cheer-uhhl!"

I heard my name loudly called. Surprised, I turned.

There, drunkenly teetering on the edge of a bar stool, was someone who looked vaguely familiar: a chubby man with shellacked ink-black hair, a short-sleeve dress shirt tucked into pleated khakis topped off with a brown braided belt that didn't match the scuffed black Sketchers he wore.

"Cheryl, right?" He stood. "Or should I say…Sweetie?"

He slurred heavily and stunk like he'd doused himself in cheap beer and expensive cologne. He could have probably immolated himself with the nearby bar matches. He came closer to us and Erin and I backed up a step.

"'Sweetie'? That's what he calls you, right? But, that's what you call him too. It doesn't really make sense. Love never does."

Erin looked at me confused, before the man closed his eyes and nodded knowingly, like he got this reaction quite a bit.

"Ah. I get it. You don't recognize me. Don't remember the IT guy. Why would you?"

I was really confused as well. Erin looked at me wondering what was up.

"I'm sorry. *Should* I know who you are?"

He leaned in close to me.

"We met just a few weeks ago. I'm Philip. I work at your boyfriend's office."

Erin smiled. "Ah…"

"Yeah, boyfriend. Secret relationship, huh? Well, not for me." He smiled toward Erin and then me. "I've been reading your emails since day one."

"You've been what…?"

"Yes, you might say emails are the love stories of lonely IT guys' lives."

On Thurs, Dec 29 at 8:56 AM, D. Satyr <d@satyr.com> wrote:

We've talked enough. I'd say it's finally time to meet. Crazy proposal, but you seem like a CRAZY girl: New Year's Eve first date?

On Thurs, Dec 29, 11:15 AM, Cheryl Sheffield <cherylo@gmail.com> wrote:

Seriously? NYE? What if I already have a hot date??? :)

On Thurs, Dec 29 at 3:44 PM, D. Satyr <d@satyr.com> wrote:

Do you?

On Thurs, Dec 29, 7:25 PM, Cheryl Sheffield <cherylo@gmail.com> wrote:

Maybe. Nothing special. Just a few girlfriends were planning to maybe go a few places with a few people. You?

On Fri, Dec 30 at 7:56 AM, D. Satyr <d@satyr.com> wrote:

You saw my Flakr profile. You know what I'll say. I'm one of those guys that will say NYE sucks. That it's "Amateur Night." Well it IS. But people that call it that are amateurs themselves. What better day to have a first date then? Let's start early before the other morons are out and about. Meet me at the subway stop on W. 4th at 7:00 and we'll walk to this little hole-in-the-wall I like.

On Thurs, Dec 30, 7:57 AM, Cheryl Sheffield <cherylo@gmail.com> wrote:

K. See you then. ;)

On Mon, Jan 2, 8:01 AM, Cheryl Sheffield <cherylo@gmail.com> wrote:

That was a pretty crazy way to ring in the New Year's, huh?

On Mon, Jan 2, 8:15 AM, D. Satyr <d@satyr.com> wrote:

Well…I can't say I've ever done it while fireworks were exploding outside my bedroom window.

> On Mon, Jan 2, 8:45 AM, Cheryl Sheffield <cherylo@gmail.com> wrote:
>
> What about sex that *technically* took place in two separate years! :)

On Mon, Jan 2, 9:23 AM, D. Satyr <d@satyr.com> wrote:

Wow, you're right! I lasted for two whole years? Man, I must have good stamina. You might have to start calling me Sting…

> On Mon, Jan 2, 10:15 AM, Cheryl Sheffield <cherylo@gmail.com> wrote:

So Sting…a message in a bottle for you: when is date #2?

On Mon, Jan 2, 4:45 PM D. Satyr <d@satyr.com> wrote:

Aren't you forward?!?!?!

> On Mon, Jan 2, 5:05 PM, Cheryl Sheffield <cherylo@gmail.com> wrote:
>
> I'm too old to be coy. :)

On Tues, Jan 3, 7:45 AM, D. Satyr <d@satyr.com> wrote:

Wait a sec? How old are you?! You said 31 on your profile. Are you lying about your age, Ms. Sheffield? ;)

> On Tues, Jan 3, 9:07 AM, Cheryl Sheffield <cherylo@gmail.com> wrote:
> Did I just get the big bad Devin Satyr to use an emoticon? ;)

On Tues, Jan 3, 3:45 PM, D. Satyr <d@satyr.com> wrote:

I guess you're just turning me into a real sweetheart, huh? Should I be scared?

On Tues, Jan 3, 5:05 PM, Cheryl Sheffield <cherylo@gmail.com> wrote:

Never again, Sweetie…

Erin looked at me.

"I can't believe you've been reading our emails! What if I reported you to him?!"

"It's my job. To ensure quality control. What if I reported you or your boyfriend to his board?"

"For what?"

"Wasting valuable company resources. On emoticons."

He winked at me, then started cracking up maniacally.

Erin and I turned and walked away, Erin now even more confused.

Then, I too started cracking up maniacally. It truly was hilarious. I was proud of our relationship, not embarrassed, nor scared. Why had I hidden it from everyone for so long? Why did I care that someone else finally knew about it? Especially a stranger. It was certainly time my real friends knew.

We returned to the booth and Erin put her hand on Les's back, touching him intentionally for the first time all night. The foray into foreplay.

Then, I immediately plopped down on Devin's lap, giving him a deep kiss, becoming publicly official.

"Hey, Sweetie."

"Hey, Sweetie."

"What's going on?"

"Wait…you two?!" exclaimed Les.

Erin looked even more shocked.

"No! This is who that IT dork was talking about? You date him, Cher?!"

Devin laughed at Erin who kept blabbering.

"This scumbag is the boyfriend? Your boyfriend?!"

"She's been dating this scumbag for the last six months." Devin smiled. "But, hey, who's keeping track?!"

"He's the best man I've ever known."

Devin smiled mockingly at Erin.

"And we're in looooove."

"But, Cheryl, what about his sordid past? All his gross stories?!"

She was pleading with me, trying to retroactively cock-block Devin. Of course she couldn't.

"We share everything with each other. I've never met such an honest guy."

"Hey! I know about her sordid past too!"

He playfully squeezed my waist.

"So…? This is it, Cher?"

"I guess it is."

"But why didn't you tell me?"

"I've been trying to for months. You've been in your own world with Joe."

"But you're not single."

"I guess that's true—I'm a single woman no longer."

I smiled at Devin.

"And, you know, I don't think I'll ever be one again. What do you think, Sweetie?"

"We're all drunk and I think…we should finally go home."

chapter thirty-one
DESCRIBING THE INDESCRIBABLE

I remember the night after our first night together. Do you remember that, Sweetie? You probably just thought you'd had another cute girl in a line of cute girls. Nothing special.

Guys never realize 'til later they're in love. That's because guys are rational, or desperately trying to be. You probably carefully analyzed things about me. Character traits, but not my character.

You always say I'm a "slight bohemian," which makes me think you don't quite understand what that word means. No, you don't need to go to an Ivy League school to know that word. Do I wear flowing clothes and hang up dream catchers in my apartment? I know you hated that one girlfriend of yours who was into astrology. I'm not, of course. I think that's stupid too.

Do you really think the fact I'm a writer and not an accountant or lawyer or teacher really matters? Do you really think it matters that I love to read, that I hate politics, that I'm apathetic toward sports? There's millions of girls like that. But you don't like them, you like me. Why do you think that is?

I remember leaving your high-rise that next night, just as the sun was setting. We'd met at sunset on New Year's Eve for our first date. We met on w. 4th Street. Now I was leaving your W. 44th Street apartment and I felt like a new woman, a different person. You'd resolved my new year before it had even begun.

You infected me with your essence from day one. And, I know I did likewise to you. You're now using emoticons and talking on the telephone for hours, holding my hand in public and going to those boring book readings I like so much.

I spun through the revolving doors and into Hell's Kitchen where I was whiplashed by the cold January 1st air. Where before I would have been bitter at its bitterness, now I relished it and even decided to walk all the way home. As I crossed town, the people walking the busy streets around me all felt so *real*. The tourists in town for the holidays, the vacationers, the celebrators. They all felt part of the latest chapter in my life story, the one that had just begun to be written the day I met you. Just a day earlier.

The clothes in the store windows sparkled. Hey, I could see myself in that sweater, those shoes. Of course it started to snow, why wouldn't it? Not coarse snowflakes that hurt, but fluffy ones that caressed my body, taking forever to fall to ground level, where they just nestled on my nose and forehead, a million little kisses, then danced on my shoulders and back, a zillion little massages. I seemed to be the only person even noticing this magic.

You don't believe an expression like "floating on air" until it happens to you, until you start floating. It's only a cliché if you've never experienced it before. But once you have, you feel sorry for any one who hasn't. And I did that New Year's Day, walking the streets, looking at all the people around me that hadn't yet found the love of their lives. Who might not ever.

Twenty-five hours before, I was a thirtysomething still trying to make it as a screenwriter. Now I was a full-fledged woman in love. At least it felt that way. Was I rushing things in my head? Maybe. But our first day had been so magical.

Twenty-four hours together.

Our *first* twenty-four hours together.

Three meals.

Dozens of drinks.

Even more hugs and kisses.

Three orgasms for you.

Four for me.

Now you would never rush things. You probably think you didn't begin falling for me until a few weeks later when I brought you to my friend's show in Greenpoint. You'd never ever go to Brooklyn you said. "Do I have to bring my passport?" you joked. You'd never ever hang with hipsters, you declared.

You said, you joked, you declared, you noted, but you know what...next thing I knew, you were flailing around to rock music inside a cramped club. I saw it in your face that night: this girl (*me*) is great. You think it was because of the fun experience. It wasn't.

It was the emotionality of the indescribable becoming describable.

What are the chances we'd meet online? What are the chances I'd think that bar was so cool? The food so good? Oddly, I wasn't feeling anything that remarkable at the start of that first date.

Sure you were cute. Sure you were kind and well-dressed and cool. You were smart, you were funny. Sure. You made me laugh several times. You seemed to have good taste in food and better in drink. Or, at least, you *liked* to drink!

I even remember you going to the bathroom and me glancing at my phone, thinking, "I'll surely be done with this date before 10:00, enough time to meet up with the girls to watch the ball drop."

But then we meandered on to that old man bar. What's it called? Oh, right, The Ear Inn. You couldn't believe I'd never been. You told me it was one of the oldest bars in New York. That longshoremen used to go there back in the 1800s and drink and fight and if any one of them was killed they just opened the back door and dumped them off a plank into the Hudson. I still think you're making that up. It doesn't say anything about that on Wikipedia.

And, sure enough, soon enough, it was 11:30 and we were in a cab making out, blowing by the packed streets of people in glittery hats and \ 2 0 1 4 / glasses, hurtling back to your apartment on the busiest night of the year.

I hadn't planned on sleeping with you that night. I never once recall looking at you and thinking, "We are definitely sleeping together tonight!" But, we definitely did. That night and well into morning.

You probably assumed we would sleep together before the date even began. Before you'd even met me in the flesh. You're so cocky.

Though, how would you know if sleeping with me was your strategy or your fate?

Whatever the case…it was magical. I thought streamers and ticker tape were going to rain down on us.

I woke up that next morning, in your bed, and though I should have had a hangover I didn't. My mind never felt clearer, but my stomach felt weird. Not sick from booze and those late night French fries we ordered in at 3 AM, but love sick.

I was a new woman, and I didn't feel like going home.

I had the world's busiest day, you don't even realize. I had so much work to do to prepare for the first week of the new year, meetings with film people out in Hollywood that could possibly change my life. But I didn't want to leave you. To your credit, you didn't pull guy rank and try to get me to leave either.

You probably liked me right from the start because I drank hard and slept with dudes on the first date.

We were in bed so long on Sunday I'm surprised our bodies didn't atrophy. That we didn't get bedsores. The only thing that got sore were our genitals (and mouths I suppose). The only body parts getting a workout during that whole time. Hugs, sex, spoon, nap, talk, Netflix, order food in, eat, laugh, laugh, and laugh.

It was the greatest day of my life.

I doubt many people would ever say the greatest day of

their life took place completely in bed, but the greatest day of my life did.

The day after the day I met you.

The second I was apart from you, riding down the elevator and going out those revolving doors, I already missed you so much. I'd only known you for one day, but I never wanted to spend another day apart from you. Luckily, I already knew I wouldn't spend many for the rest of my life.

I thought my life was fine. Actually, it was pretty great. I had tons of friends. Tons of things to do. Four days a week I had coffee with a friend. Three days a week I grabbed a lunch. Dinners and drinks, pretty much every single weeknight. Birthday parties and events. Happy hours every Friday. Village brunches with the gal and gay pals on Saturdays and Sundays. I didn't need a man. I didn't need you. I had men in my life. Two to three dates per week. I wasn't exactly a slut but I never particularly struggled meeting men. Never struggled getting asked out.

Were they the greatest men? No. But many of them, *most* of them, were pretty damn decent. Handsome and fit. Well-educated and smart. Some were even witty. All were pretty fun to be around and to do things with. They were all solid in bed too and liked to be in bed with me if you don't mind me saying so.

In another world, maybe I would have even married one of these guys. But then I met you.

And now I realize:

Those nights out, those dinners and drinks, brunches and lunches and coffees? I was just biding my time.

Biding my time 'til I could meet you.

Now, when I'm with you, I feel whole. I feel so happy.

Now, even when I'm alone, I'm not alone. Because you're always with me. In my thoughts, in my mind, in my heart.

Devin, we aren't perfect for each other because we have similar personalities; we are perfect for each other because of those things you can't describe. Those feelings you give me in my mind, stomach, and...*lower* regions.

No one ever caused me to have those feelings before, but

you. That's why we are together. That's why we are in love.

I'm drunk, I'm rambling.

Let's get engaged, let's move to LA.

I'm so glad to hear that and you're right: Les doesn't need you here any more.

Did you see them though? They were stunned. I told you we should have told them earlier. OK, we stole Erin's thunder for the night. She was gonna sleep with Les. Shocker! Maybe she still will. I think it's more strategy than fate in her mind, though maybe not his. But you'd know better than me. Will they fall in love? Who knows?

I hope so.

Or, I hope not.

I just hope they each find who's right for them even if it isn't *them*.

I hope Erin finds the man that makes her feel like you make me feel. Like I make *you* feel.

I love you, Sweetie.

You'll never be single again.

Now tell me about everything I missed tonight.

continue the story by picking up

THE GUIDE FOR A SINGLE MAN

AVAILABLE NOW AT FGPRESS.COM
AND OTHER RETAILERS

THE GUIDE FOR A SINGLE MAN PREVIEW

chapter one

FUCK SEX

"Sex-ed really did a terrible job."

"Of what?"

"Of educating us. About sex."

"We were in sixth grade."

"So you remember?"

"Sort of."

"What was it? 1990?"

"OK. We were twelve."

"Yeah. I remember standing behind you in the boys' line. Nervously eyeing the girls beside us, like we were headed for the electric chair."

"I wasn't nervous."

"Of course you weren't, Devin. You always knew what to do with girls before any of us even knew what we could do with girls."

"I guess."

"That's just how it was. You really don't remember?"

I thought back to that sex-ed assembly. I recalled being split into separate groups. I guess they assumed the girls would be self-conscious when shown filmstrip fallopian tubes. That us boys would act immature upon learning what the pituitary gland actually does.

At that age, amongst the genders, you cannot make the pubic public.

So they threw us boys into the cafétorium where we did indeed laugh at illustrated ball sacks. Rolling around on the linoleum floor, shoving each other in manic glee, continually repeating the word "pubes."

Meanwhile, the girls were in the band room watching a '60s-era slide show that included hundreds of images of giant, erect penises. This was revealed later that day during lunch by Tricia Younger. She proudly noted to me that every girl had her mouth agape except her. Which was ironic as Tricia would quickly become the kind of girl who always gaped open her mouth for a giant, erect penis.

The boys assembly was run by a local gynecologist and amateur bodybuilder named Dr. Van Dyke. We quite obviously called him Dr. Veiny Dick.

"All y'all will soon learn, once you get a li'l older, ain't nothin' more beautiful than *coitus!*" he loudly proclaimed.

Coitus was a word we didn't know at the time, just like *fornication*, *intercourse*, and *fellatio*. Fancy words for what we yet didn't know were un-fancy acts. Still, after the assembly, we immediately circled all those words in the classroom *Webster's*.

The girls assembly was run by our dumpy school nurse, Miss Holmes. We quite obviously called her Miss Homo. Tricia giggled in reporting Miss Homo struggled to get through any sentence with the word copulate in it. We counted it up later: the McGraw Hill Sexual Health Instructor's Guide, Volume 15 (©1979) had 427 mentions of "copulate," "copulation," or "copulating" in it.

Though both assemblies were just an hour, we learned a lifetime of useless shit from Veiny Dick:

"Nocturnal emissions are nothing to lose sleep over."

"No, anal sex is not considered a legitimate expression of love."

"*Uhn-uh*, Justin Martin, you *cannot* use Saran Wrap as a prophylactic!"

It was the same useless shit boys and girls had been taught since the beginning of time. Or, at least since sex-ed assemblies became prominent in the public education system and class clowns like Justin Martin asked questions simply meant to make classmates laugh.

"So, yeah, I guess I remember that assembly," I told Les.

"Good. Because I would imagine everyone in America—except those home-schooled weirdos—remembers a similar sex-ed experience."

"It's part of 'growing up.'"

"That's my point!" Les lightly backhanded my shoulder.

"What's that?"

"That maybe it *shouldn't* be."

"You want to eliminate sex-ed?"

"I never said that."

"You just insinuated."

"I'm not some ultra-conservative creationist wackjob who believes dinosaurs helped Moses part the Red Sea."

It was almost shocking our shitty middle American school hadn't taught us that.

Les continued, "Look, Devin, what I'm simply saying is, they really need to change sex-ed. Make it more…realistic."

"And how would they do that?"

"By being more honest."

"No one's honest about sex."

"Exactly! And that's the problem. *The* point of sex-ed was never to teach us anything useful. It's never been to sexually educate children."

"OK. Then what was the point?"

"'The point,' Devin? The point was to scare children away from ever *fucking*!"

Les looked me in the eyes, dead seriously.

"And how do they do that?"

He counted with his fingers:

"By evoking religion,

 "with doomsday thoughts of pregnancy,

 "oh, and don't forget, frequently showing pictures of disgusting dick diseases."

He was kind of right. Back in 1990, Miss Homo preached to Tricia Younger and the other girls:

"Thou shalt not couple unless in love. And married. Under God. Jesus, too. It says so in the Bible. Genesis, I believe. Look it up, ladies. Minister Simpson says it's all there."

For some reason the separation of church and state has never seemed to matter if it keeps children from sticking their wieners into things or having wieners stuck into them.

At the same time Miss Homo was lying to the little girls, Veiny Dick was ranting to us boys:

"Babies having babies?! Now how ya gonna find a babysitter on prom night? You are the babysitter, bucko!"

After that line Justin Martin cracked a joke about losing *his* virginity to his babysitter and was immediately removed from the room. Of course, Justin was a father by our senior year and, as best as I can judge from Facebook, now has three children from two different women. He traded in "class clown" for "bartender at a Pizzeria Uno in the mall."

"Of course, we also had to watch never-ending slides"—CLICK, CLICK, CLICK—"of inflamed genitalia"—RED DICK, OOZING DICK, BUBBLING DICK.

"That flaming dick was seared into my brain."

"Still, it didn't work, Devin, did it? All that shit—religion, pregnancy, disgusting dick diseases—*didn't* work! Not for Justin Martin, not for Tricia Younger, not for you, and certainly not for me. You know why?"

"Why?"

"Because there's nothing we crave more than sex. Pregnancy, disease, and God be damned!"

"So..."

"So...what Homo and Veiny Dick should have said, if they truly wanted to deter us from sex, was something like: 'Don't have sex, kiddos, because: you'll *never* be able to get enough of it!'"

I knew where he was coming from. Like most men, my best friend Les had had his sexual highs and sexual lows. Those certain times women—or more likely, A (singular) woman—couldn't get enough of him, and those certain times when he was as hard up as a man could possibly be. Hard up with a hard-on. A terrible way to live one's life, I've always told him. Yet, he always told me, sadly, far too much about his sex life.

LESLEY MANN
Lifetime Statistics

SEXUAL DEBUT	May 25, 1996
TOTAL PARTNERS	11
TOTAL PERFORMANCES	328 (over 235 days)
LONGEST HOT STREAK	9 straight days (8/14–22/09)
LONGEST COLD STREAK	280 straight days (3/9–11/5/03)
LIFETIME AVERAGE	235 / 6,044 = 0.039
FRANCHISES	0

A guy his age could have done better in life. A guy his age should have done better by now. He had to know this. He continued ranting.

"'Don't have sex because, even though it's the most important thing in the world, you'll rarely get to participate in it!'"

For him, that was true. A mere 4% of his days since becoming sexually active had been days Les had actually *been* active. Assuming each act, foreplay to finish, generously averaged ten minutes long, then the most important thing in the world was something Les only got to participate in 0.00001% of his life.

Aaron Goldfarb | PREVIEW

"Even when the going's been good, Devin. Even when Jenn or Alice or *fucking* Katey couldn't get enough of me. Early on in our relationships of course. Even if she'd just had sex with me one hundred days in a row? That one-hundred-and-first day when she *didn't*, when she just rolled over and went to bed and I'd be left tossing and turning until I was finally forced to turn over and toss it? That always felt like the *worst* day of my life."

Women didn't realize how pathetic guys like Les could be. How getting a sexual advance rebuffed could absolutely crush their fragile male egos.

"Devin, why didn't Van Dyke just say: 'Don't ever have sex, boys, because it'll make you too self-conscious!'"

Les looked at me sadly.

"Especially when you're not having any. 'Why won't someone fuck me? Am I ugly? Getting fat? Do I smell? Am I too poor? Bad in bed?!' The best thing, I now realize, about me being in relationships, is that I lose all that shitty self-consciousness."

When Les was single, he was always obsessing over things. Constantly worrying about his male relatives who were bald (father, grandfather, two uncles) and how early they'd gone (19, 22, 21, 23), and being certain he too would be bald one day. The idiot used to waste $90 a month on Minoxidil, even though he had a head of hair thicker than the rough at Augusta National.

"Should I go back to the Rogaine? I wonder if that's why Jenn dumped me." Les tried to examine his hairline in the bar's dirty wall mirror. "Did I just become too relaxed in our relationship?"

"That's not why, Les."

Single men were so much sharper about the world around them. Most men's brains became mush when they were in a relationship. Jenn had turned Les's brain into mashed potatoes.

"If I ever get another girlfriend, I'm going to have to stay sharp, not become too relaxed, you know? I don't want a Jenn situation to ever happen again. 'Don't have sex, kids, because…'"

He paused.

"Because…?"

"Because…because…because. I got nothing."

Les slumped down on his barstool, completely spent.

"I can't stop thinking about Jenn. Three hours ago she was my girlfriend. Now she's just a memory." He exhaled. "'Don't have sex because: it'll dominate your thoughts.' 'Don't have sex because: you'll grow to hate yourself.' 'Don't have sex because: it'll make you screw over your friends just to screw all over some questionable girl you just met.'"

"What's that?"

Les lifted himself up and looked me in the eyes, apologetic.

"Devin, I have to apologize. I can't count the number of times over the years we'd be talking to the same girl and the second you went to take a leak, I swarmed on her."

Les shook his head in disgust at himself.

"It's OK, bud." I usually went to the bathroom simply to stick those women with Les.

"'Don't have sex because: it drives you to treat friends as rivals.'"

Les bent his head down toward his lap. Even though he'd only had a single beer, I was starting to get concerned he might yack.

"'Don't have sex, you little bastards, because: it'll make you physically ill.'"

He looked back up at me, his face turning pale.

"'Don't have sex because: you'll soon need it just to validate your pathetic existence.' I am so pathetic, Devin. So pathetic! If I had the chance, I know I'd fall to my knees like a sinner at the Pearly Gates, staring upward at a massive vagina consuming me, crying out, pleading: 'Please tell me I'm good, Saint Beaver! Please loooove me!!!!'"

I laughed, thinking Les was trying to be funny for once. He wasn't. A few bros at the end of the bar glanced over at Les's histrionics.

"I am so fucking pathetic. 'Don't have sex,' they should have said, 'because: it will…eventually…*ruin your life.*'"

Les was shaking. I put my hand on his back to steady him.

"I can just see myself later tonight, sitting in my empty apartment with a fifth of whatever, composing a note:

> DEAR JENN'S VAGINA,
>
> I HAVE DECIDED TO KILL MYSELF BECAUSE YOU WILL NO LONGER FUCK ME...

I bit my tongue. Les could really be crazy sometimes.

"The misery that comes with being an adult in love. Is it even worth it?! I'm not so sure anymore."

"It *is*."

"Sometimes I envy eunuchs. My stupid dick has just led me like a divining rod toward a gold mine of misery."

"That's not true, bud."

"But it is! I was such a happy boy growing up. You know that! And, then, I wasn't. Because girls came into my life. Girls I wanted, but couldn't get. My mind told me I needed them, my body told me I had to have them, and every other force in the world conspired against me so I couldn't get them."

"Well, it's sometimes hard to be an adult looking for love."

"Or sex. That's all I'm saying, man. All Veiny Dick had to say to us was, 'Don't have sex…because it will totally ruin your fucking life.' Without getting a disease, or accidentally getting any one pregnant, or even angering God, sex will still ruin your motherfucking life."

Les gripped my shoulders with both his hands, pulling me in close.

"It's ruined mine, Devin. *Fuck sex*. That's all they needed to teach us in sex-ed. *Fuck sex*. The assembly could have lasted just two minutes. *FUCK. Sex.*"

I didn't know what else to do but give him a hug. The bros

at the end of the bar watched closely. Les broke from my clutches and pulled back.

"But maybe I'm just saying this…because I'm pretty sure…I'm never going to get laid again."

ACKNOWLEDGMENTS

I would like to thank Brad Feld, Dane McDonald, and the team at FG Press for giving me this incredible opportunity. This includes Sandy Grason, Kevin Kane, Eugene Wan, and Dave Heal. I would like to thank the great Craig T. Wood for spurring the idea for these works and Phil Simon for setting me up with FG Press. And I would like to thank Betsy for now giving me *The Guide for a Married Man*.

ABOUT THE AUTHOR

Aaron Goldfarb is the author of *How to Fail: The Self-Hurt Guide*, the 2010 satirical novel that has sold over 100,000 copies. Aaron was born in Manhattan, raised in Oklahoma City, and attended Syracuse University's Newhouse School. In addition to *How to Fail*, Aaron has a short story collection about "the sexes, sex, and sexiness in New York," *The Cheat Sheet* (2011), as well as a book of his collected drinking essays, *Drunk Drinking* (2012). A noted craft beer and spirits expert, Aaron writes about those subjects and more on a weekly basis for *Esquire*. He is also a frequent contributor to *Playboy*, MTV, and *Draft Magazine* and currently has several film and television projects in various stages of development. He lives in New York City and can be contacted via email aaron@aarongoldfarb.com or on Twitter @aarongoldfarb.

ABOUT FG PRESS

Thank you for supporting the future of publishing! We are FG Press, a small group of entrepreneurs crazy enough to think that we can change the world of publishing. We do this by putting our authors first, and by creating a community of involvement between authors, editors, designers, and readers.

FG Press was founded in late 2013 by the team at Foundry Group. As venture capitalists and authors, we believe there is a clear path of innovation away from the current publishing model—one that is defined by one-sided royalty splits, cumbersome bureaucracy, poor transparency, and ineffective support—to one that can better serve authors and readers.

Welcome to the family. Send us an email (info@fgpress.com) to let us know how we're doing and we'll send you something awesome in return (like a coupon code for another one of our titles).

Join the conversation amongst our authors and readers in The Parlour at parlour.fgpress.com and follow us on Twitter and Facebook. Thank you!

CPSIA information can be obtained at www.ICGtesting.com
Printed in the USA
BVOW02s1005050115

381964BV00001B/6/P